"Stay for dinner, Merry, and [illegible] ve you home," Shane said softly in his [illegible] h, deep voice.

"No thanks." She took two sensible steps toward the door. "I don't think it's the best idea for me to be here with you. In fact, I'm certain it isn't."

"Why?" he asked, a grin twitching the corners of his mouth. "Besides, you haven't seen the rest of my place yet. It'll only take a minute."

Merle glanced at him. True to his promise, he hadn't made anything resembling a pass. He hadn't even touched her. "All right, show me the rest."

He pointed out the features of the houseboat, the guest room, the bathroom. "The master bedroom is the last room on the hallway," he said, his voice low and detached. "My bedroom." He stood aside for her to enter.

It seemed oddly warm on the boat. Her face was flushed, though her skin was puckered in goose bumps. She looked inside the room, and the first and only thing she saw was the bed—his bed.

That was it, that was all she could tolerate. Whirling around, she crashed into Shane, who threw out his arms to catch her. "Sorry," he said, his voice husky, his lips against her hair. "You okay?"

"No!" Her face was pressed against his chest, her lips buried in the puff of hair at the base of his throat. His heart thundered under her ear. Every nerve in her body had come alive, and desperate need fueled her actions.

Throwing her arms around his neck, she pulled his mouth down to hers. He met her lips with bruising intensity. She moaned deep in her throat. She'd waited so long, so long for this moment, and she couldn't get enough of him. . . .

WHAT ARE *LOVESWEPT* ROMANCES?

They are stories of true romance and touching emotion. We believe those two very important ingredients are constants in our highly sensual and very believable stories in the *LOVESWEPT* line. Our goal is to give you, the reader, stories of consistently high quality that may sometimes make you laugh, sometimes make you cry, but are always fresh and creative and contain many delightful surprises within their pages.

Most romance fans read an enormous number of books. Those they truly love, they keep. Others may be traded with friends and soon forgotten. We hope that each *LOVESWEPT* romance will be a treasure—a "keeper." We will always try to publish

LOVE STORIES YOU'LL NEVER FORGET
BY AUTHORS YOU'LL ALWAYS REMEMBER

The Editors

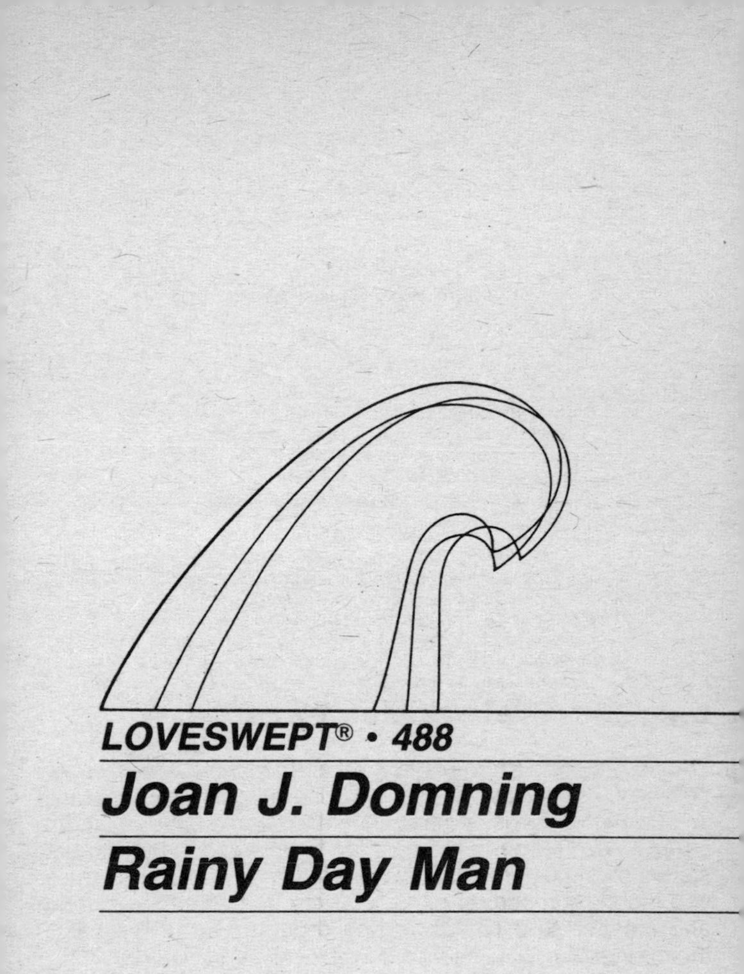

LOVESWEPT® • 488

Joan J. Domning

Rainy Day Man

BANTAM BOOKS
NEW YORK • TORONTO • LONDON • SYDNEY • AUCKLAND

RAINY DAY MAN

A Bantam Book / August 1991

ISBN 0-553-44182-5

Published simultaneously in the United States and Canada

Bantam Books are published by Bantam Books, a division of Bantam Doubleday Dell Publishing Group, Inc. Its trademark, consisting of the words "Bantam Books" and the portrayal of a rooster, is Registered in U.S. Patent and Trademark Office and in other countries. Marca Registrada. Bantam Books, 666 Fifth Avenue, New York, New York 10103.

PRINTED IN THE UNITED STATES OF AMERICA

OPM 0 9 8 7 6 5 4 3 2 1

For my very special friend,
Carla Willison

Rainy Day Man

Prologue

Merle Pierce left the BART station and made a high-heeled dash through the San Francisco March rain, her face flushed with anticipation and happiness. When she stepped into the foyer of the coffeehouse, a young woman in tailored slacks and a blue plaid blazer shot up off a deacon's bench and stared at her with large brown eyes that were a perfect match for her own.

"Ms. Pierce . . . ?" the young woman asked uncertainly.

"Yes," Merle whispered, numbed by the realization that her dream had finally come true. "And you must be Ellen Ehrhart."

"I'm Ellen."

Merle ached to gather her daughter into her arms, but they were strangers. Another woman had raised her child. So many questions had tormented her since the adoption, twenty-three years before. What kind of life had she ordained for her baby? Fear of the answer drained the color out of her face.

After they'd shaken hands, Merle studied Ellen hungrily. It was a relief to see that all she'd inherited from Shane was his black hair, though hers was smooth and straight where his had been a curly mop.

She couldn't have borne seeing him in her daughter's face.

She was verging on tears when the hostess flounced up, chattering about the bad weather as she led them through the coffeehouse to a table by a rain-streaked window. By the time the woman left, Merle had regained her composure. "It was quite a surprise when my father's lawyer phoned to say you wanted to meet me," she said softly, taking off her wet raincoat.

"I expect it must have been," Ellen said, sitting down at the table. "I wasn't sure you'd want me to find you."

"Want you to! I leaped at the chance. I've been so looking forward to seeing you."

"Me too. I've been curious about you all my life."

Tears threatened again. Merle turned to look in a mirror surrounded by shelves of knickknacks, and fussed with her hair. In control again, she sat down at the table. "Meeting like this for the first time is a little awkward, isn't it?"

Ellen blew out a breath. "Is it ever. I'm not even sure what to call you. Ms. Pierce seems so stilted."

"Why don't you call me Merle? Then maybe we can settle down and get to know each other. How would that be?"

"I'd like that." A full smile lit Ellen's face for the first time as her reserve lightened.

Merle stared at her, eyes wide, mouth ajar. It was Shane's smile, crooked on the right side, showing even white teeth. She snapped her mouth shut, thinking how idiotic it was to be so shaken over the smallest reminder of a long-lost boyfriend.

A waitress placed mugs, a pot of French vanilla flavored coffee, and a bowl of mints on the table. After she left, Merle took a deep breath and said, "Tell me all about yourself, Ellen. Where did you grow up? What do you do? Who *are* you?"

Ellen shrugged, stirring cream into her coffee. "I

grew up in Palo Alto—I still live there. I'll graduate with a degree in engineering in June. I've always been something of a math whiz. I like things well organized." Shane's smile bloomed on her face again when she held out her left hand to display a diamond solitaire. "And I'm going to be married on the last Saturday in July."

"Are you really, love?" Merle said softly, covering her regret over having missed all her daughter's special moments. "That's wonderful."

Ellen nodded, her smooth black hair swaying. "My fiancé and I have our entire life until death do us part planned out. That's why I wanted to meet you. We intend to have children, so I need a medical history of my biological family. I wouldn't think of conceiving if there were any genetic weaknesses in my background."

"You really are looking ahead, aren't you?" Merle crossed her knees restlessly, wondering where this methodical daughter had come from, when she'd made such a mess of her own life. "I had a genetic workup done several years ago at an infertility clinic. I'll pass it on to you."

Ellen leaned forward curiously. "I assume you were trying to get pregnant. Did it work?"

"Unfortunately it didn't. I don't have any children . . . other children." Merle pressed her palm against her chest. She'd wanted to be a mother so badly; the disappointment was still sharp, like a knife slicing her heart.

Ellen gazed at her sympathetically. "That seems so unfair!"

"Life isn't always fair, I guess." Merle moved her hand up to smooth rebellious platinum blond tendrils off her forehead. Then she leaned forward and said intensely, "It broke my heart to give you up, I want you to know that. And now I've got to ask. I have to know. Did you have a happy childhood? Were your adoptive parents good to you?"

Ellen smiled tenderly. "Oh, yes, very happy. Mother and Daddy were darlings. They brought me up with a nice solid balance of guidance, fun, and love."

Relief flushed through Merle. "Oh, I'm glad. I was so afraid—" Her voice caught in her throat.

"No, they were wonderful to me. But they were middle-aged when they got me, and they both died young. Mother when I was eighteen, and Daddy just a year ago. I miss them a lot." Ellen closed her eyes and put her hand over her mouth for a moment, then glanced up. "You gave me two precious gifts. My life and my parents."

Tears sprang to Merle's eyes. "Thank you for telling me that."

"This is getting soppy, isn't it?" Ellen said with an embarrassed laugh.

"It's on the brink." Merle laughed, too, and wiped at her eyes with her napkin.

Ellen unwrapped a mint, tucked it into her cheek, and sipped coffee, studying Merle over the rim of the mug. She noted how youthful her mother was, how understated her beauty. In a cocoa-brown suit, with pearls at her neck and ears, Merle was elegant. "You must have been awfully young when you had me. I hope you loved my biological father at least a little bit."

To Merle's dismay, a resurgence of the anger and sense of betrayal she'd felt so many years ago washed over her. She tried to laugh the feeling off. "I was the ripe old age of sixteen, and I thought I had the love of the century."

Then, what she'd been dreading happened. A precise image of Shane Halloran burst into her mind. She could see him clearly, a big, teasing eighteen-year-old, with blue eyes that could spark her body to life with a glance. And that smile! Even the memory of Shane's smile had the power to weaken her knees.

She shook her head slowly. "We must have been so unsuited for each other. He was a rabble-rousing sixties-era hippie, and I was a quiet, prim girl. I have no idea what he saw in me, but I literally worshiped him."

Merle gazed at rivulets of rain streaming like tears down the windowpane beside the table. "The war in Vietnam was going on and on, so he was drafted into the army as soon as he graduated from high school. It was a case of out of sight, out of mind. He lost interest in me, and I was left stranded, pregnant, and terrified." She brushed at her suit jacket, as if she could brush away the hurt she still felt.

After a moment Ellen asked, "Have you seen him since?"

"Never! I made darn good and certain we didn't meet again. Luckily we don't travel in the same circles." Merle picked up her mug and sipped from it.

"Do you know where he lives? I want to meet him too."

She sputtered when her swallow of coffee went down the wrong way. "Good Lord, Ellen, you can't contact him! He doesn't even know about you! I tried to tell him years ago, but I have absolutely no intention of breaking the news to him at this late date."

Ellen blithely waved a hand. "I'll ring him up and feel him out. If he isn't receptive, I won't pursue it."

Merle pulled at the pearls around her neck as if they were choking her. "Let me try to explain my position. I work for a teen magazine—*Youngest Sister.* In fact, I write an advice column for adolescent girls, and—"

Ellen broke in, "When I was a kid I subscribed to *Youngest Sister*! You can't be Miss Merry of the 'Ask Miss Merry' column?"

Merle felt half-embarrassed to admit it. "I'm afraid so."

Ellen's face lit up. "Oh, my gosh, my friends and I used to consider you the final word on sex and boys!"

"Did you really? Well, I'm glad I could contribute at least that much to your childhood." Merle smiled, and then she frowned, trying to pick her words tactfully. "But if you know who Miss Merry is, then you must see how vulnerable I am. I'm absolutely delighted that I've found you again, darling—please believe that. But if the media should catch wind of you and me—and especially who your father is—well, it could mean disaster."

"Oh?" Ellen leaned forward with bright, curious eyes. "Who *is* my biological father?"

Merle bent her head and spread her hands out flat on the table, as if she could ward off the name—the man. But she knew Ellen had a right to know. She looked up, sighing. "I suppose you've heard of Shane Halloran. He seems to turn up in the local papers and TV news reports every so often."

"Shane Halloran!" Ellen reared back in her chair and gave a ringing laugh. "*My* biological parents are Miss Merry and Shane Halloran?"

Merle sighed. "It really isn't a bit funny."

"I'm sorry—no, it isn't. But you'll have to admit it's intriguing. My mother writes advice for lovelorn girls, and my father is a legal advocate for underage prostitutes."

"So intriguing, the media would just love it." Merle sighed again.

"Yes, but you do understand that I have to get a medical history of his family from him," Ellen said with a determined set to her chin. "Don't worry, I'll be very discreet. There won't be any repercussions." She glanced at her watch. "Oh, darn, I have to leave. I've got a class in a half an hour." She jumped up and grabbed her purse. "We've got to get together soon. I'll call, okay?"

Merle got up, said good-bye to Ellen, then dropped back in her chair. It seemed unreal—she'd finally met her daughter. Her guilt and fears had been put to rest. She felt fulfilled and happy.

But while one side of Merle's mind warned, *Don't expect too much*, the other side sent up a silent plea,

Please, please, let my daughter like me a little bit. She knew she could never be Ellen's mother, but oh how she yearned at least to be her friend. If a friendship between them was meant to be, it was Ellen's place to initiate it, she decided.

Suddenly thoughts of Shane popped into her mind. Groaning, she leaned her elbows on the table and anxiously covered her face with her hands. What would he say when Ellen contacted him?

"Oh, don't be an *idiot!*" Merle exclaimed aloud, turning heads at the next table. What could he do? At the very worst he'd send Ellen flying off with a denial, at best he'd be curious and interested. Either way, she suspected he'd try to contact her, and that was what worried her.

One

Dear Miss Merry,

I'm thirteen years old and this boy wants to go out with me. I never had a boyfriend before and I'm scared. What am I going to say to him? What if he wants to kiss me? What do I do if he wants to go farther than a kiss?

Desperate

Dear Desperate,

How exciting, love. Your first boyfriend will live forever in your heart. Talk to him about school, the other kids, or your pets. If he wants to kiss you, enjoy. But if he wants to go beyond a kiss, say no—loud and clear—or you may build regrets instead of the joyful memories you deserve.

Miss Merry

On Saturday, three days after she had met her daughter, Merle floundered down the steep, muddy hill into which her split-level home had been built. The sky had finally cleared and the sun was shining.

But if another storm came up, there was a strong possibility the entire hillside would go, taking her house with it.

So she'd tied her pale gold hair up into a ponytail, donned jeans, a gray sweatshirt, and rubber boots, and had prepared to put a makeshift raincoat over the slide area. Pressing her hands against her back, she looked to the summit, wondering how she'd manage the huge roll of plastic.

A frisson of anxiety tightened her skin when she saw a man sitting on a motorcycle in her driveway. He was leaning with one hand on each handgrip, long legs splayed out on either side of the cycle, as if he'd been watching her for some time. The warbling of catbirds and hum of traffic on the freeway below the hill had masked the sound of his arrival.

His leather jacket, gloves, and helmet were black. His face was hidden behind a smoked visor, but she instinctively knew his identity. Shane Halloran had developed a love affair with motorcycles as soon as he'd learned to drive.

She knew he'd come about Ellen, but as far as she was concerned, he was twenty-three years too late. She didn't want to talk to him. She glanced frantically toward her neighbor's house, some two acres away. Running wouldn't solve anything, she realized. Taking a deep breath, she climbed back up the slippery slope, her complexion turning pink from apprehension and exertion.

When Merle reached the driveway, her visitor toed down the kickstand of the cycle, dismounted, and took off his helmet. Once Shane had looked rangy, unfinished. But now, at forty-one, his face was forceful, tanned, and rugged, with dynamic character lines. His black hair was shot with silver but still curly, his haircut just long enough to make a statement. His eyes were still an odd light-blue color, unblinking between thick black lashes as he watched her walk toward him.

"Hullo, Merry," he said, his voice wrapping like masculine velvet around the nickname he'd given her so many years before.

"Hello, Shane." She felt lost in time.

To her surprise, anger darkened his face. "Why didn't you tell me about Ellen?" he questioned, getting right to the point.

What did he expect her to say? She lifted her hands, palms up. "You were gone."

"That's no excuse for not telling me! I had every legal right to know you were pregnant with my baby. I should have had equal say in what happened to her."

Merle planted her fists on her hips. "For Pete's sake, Shane! I was only sixteen years old. How can you expect me to have handled a situation like that with any maturity? My parents took over and told me what to do."

"And they didn't exactly worship the earth I walked on, did they?"

She leaped to their defense, though she'd never truly forgiven them herself. "They were only trying to bring me up carefully in a crazy world, and you went out of your way to act like some depraved hippie. Besides, they were right—just what they'd warned me about happened."

"That didn't make it any less my right to know about the baby I had fathered. Merry, we could have—" He broke off and bit his lip.

Merle stared at him, amazed that he was so emotional about it. "*What* could we have done? Gotten married and brought up a baby, young as we were?" If only . . . if only. Merle turned and looked away toward Mount Diablo at the east end of the valley, her large brown eyes filling with tears.

Shane blew out a breath, puffing his cheeks. "You're right, of course, it was an impossible situation. And it happened a million years ago. It's just that Ellen popped up out of nowhere, and . . . well, I felt cheated, that's all."

Nodding, she rubbed a knuckle against each eye, reluctant to let him see how much she'd cared. "That's the way I feel too. My parents insisted adoption was the only logical route, but . . ."

He stripped his gloves off, one finger at a time, and laid them on the cycle seat. Then he looked up at her, his gaze moving over her face as if searching for something he'd lost. "It's been a long time—how are you?"

The touch of his eyes inhibited her. "Fine, and you?"

"Fine," he answered formally.

Then he spread his arms and hid his deeper emotions behind banter. "What you sees is what you gets." That wonderful lopsided, toothy grin blossomed on his face. "I don't know what I thought I'd find when I came here, but I didn't expect to see you making mud pies."

She stared at him for a moment, stunned by the reemergence of her old beloved, teasing Shane. A breeze whipped whisps of hair around cheeks that had turned suddenly warm. Bending over, she beat at the mud on her jeans and wondered why he'd had to visit at a time when she was wearing her worst grubbies. She stood up again and pushed tendrils of platinum hair back into her ponytail. "I suppose I look ghastly."

"Hardly." His gaze moved like blue crystalline fire down her body, and up to her face again. "You haven't changed a bit since we were kids, Merry."

"It'd be a sad testimony to my life if I hadn't changed since I was sixteen." She glanced at him for a fraction of a second, looking for signs of the boy she'd known. Once his body had been whipcord slim. Now he was broader in the shoulders, stockier in the torso—and sexier than ever.

To her horror, the almost primal desire she'd once

felt for him surged to life again. Her voice sounded a little desperate when she said, "I might have hoped to pick up a little maturity if nothing else in twenty-three years."

He grinned as if he knew how he was affecting her, then asked, "Why exactly *are* you wallowing in the mud?"

Relieved that he'd changed the subject, she pointed. "See that slide area? I'm afraid the top of the hill will go with it, including my house. I want to cover it with plastic to keep the rain from soaking in, but it's a bigger job than I'd anticipated."

Shane stood beside the roll of plastic and shoved his fingers in his back pockets, looking down the hillside. "If you let the house slide, it'd end up right by the freeway and the BART tracks. You'd shorten your commute by several minutes."

It was a deadpan observation. She hooked two fingers through her beltloops and answered, "I seldom drive in that insane traffic, and the BART trains don't make unscheduled stops. Besides, with my luck I'd probably end up *on* the tracks, not by them."

"You're still quick with the lip for a quiet kid, aren't you?" He laughed and ran his fingers through his hair, tousling the curls. "Do you need help?"

"No! Well, probably, but I can hire someone." She wished he'd just go away and stop stirring up the past.

"That's okay, I haven't anything better to do."

Shane took off his leather jacket and folded it over the seat of his cycle. His pale blue T-shirt had the logo Life's a Beach in black letters and fit his muscular chest like a hug. The round neck was stretched out and showed a good mat of black chest hair; at eighteen he'd only had a patch in the middle of his chest. Merle winced at her reaction and tried to delete the memory from her mind.

Hefting the roll of plastic onto his shoulder, he picked his way down the steep, slippery hill to where the thick layer of topsoil had slid, taking the wild brush, grass, and flowers with it. "You hold this end," he said to Merle when she reached his side.

Merle knelt on her corner, sitting back on her rubber boots, while he unrolled the plastic to the far end of the slide and cut it. Each on an end, they unfolded it into a clear shining field. When he walked back toward her, she noticed he was limping. "Did you hurt yourself?" she asked.

His reaction to her innocent question was startling—all expression faded from his eyes and face. "It's nothing new. Compliments of my tour of duty in Nam. I took a shell in the leg."

The idea of Shane hurt and in pain was another thought Merle had to fight off. "I'm sorry."

"No need to be sorry now, it was a long time ago."

He hunkered down on his heels—so close to Merle, she could smell the citrus scent of his aftershave—and drove a wooden peg into the plastic with a vicious blow of the mallet. "The wound was nothing compared to the damned hard time I had forgiving you for dumping me after I went into the army," he said, his voice quiet and even.

Her dark brows shot up over puzzled brown eyes. "What *are* you talking about?"

"I'm saying everything was so lovey-dovey before I left—I wish I'd known it was one-sided." He rested his elbows on his cocked knees and stared down at the mallet dangling from his hand. "The least you could have done was write me a Dear John letter."

Merle jumped up and glared at him. "Shane Halloran, you're conveniently changing the past to suit yourself. I never quit writing to you! I wrote and wrote, long after you quit writing to me."

"Well, I didn't see any sign of your letters at mail call." He stood up to tower over her, his eyes flashing. "And when I came back on my first leave, I found out you'd left. Zip, you were gone."

She crossed her arms angrily. "I was gone because

when my parents found out I was pregnant, they sent me back east to live with my aunt and uncle."

"Then how come I didn't get a letter telling me something as important as that?"

"I sent one—lots and lots of them."

He pinched his lips shut and backed out of the spat by erasing the hurt and anger from his face. "Why the devil are we bickering like a couple of kids over ancient history?"

"I haven't the faintest idea." Merle looked toward the valley again, until she'd brought her emotions under control, then turned back toward him. "If neither of us quit writing, it sounds as if we were the victims of a cosmic joke or something."

"If not that, victims of the post office." Shane pursed his lips. "The message being . . . what? That we're lucky we didn't get married, if we're still acting like kids at forty?"

She wrinkled her nose. "You're forty, I'm not."

"Are you trying to stir up another fight?" He grinned and tapped her gently on the shoulder with the mallet.

Merle studied Shane curiously as he bent over and unrolled another length of plastic, digging in the heels of his boots to present her with a nice, leisurely view of his shapely rear. When she remembered he had a mole on the right cheek, she tore her gaze away. All the feelings she'd worked so hard to bury seemed to be buzzing up like ills out of Pandora's box. The man was transforming her into an erotic, high-strung woman she didn't even recognize.

He duck-walked along the plastic, setting pegs, his shoulder muscles bunching as he brought the mallet down. "It's hard to comprehend that I have an adult daughter," he said when he reached her.

Merle pulled her sweatshirt down over slim, girlish hips. "Are you saying it makes you feel your age to have a child almost a quarter of a century old?"

"Did you *have* to put it that way?" He rubbed a

forearm across his black hair. "Makes every gray hair itch."

He sat back on his heels and looked up at Merle. "Catch me up—what happened in your life after the baby was born?"

She turned quickly away and watched a BART train slide silently past below her hill like a white snake. Given the choice, she'd opt for walking tightrope on the electric third rail rather than admit to Shane how terrible the pain and grief of losing him had been. Glossing over the surface history would have to do, she decided.

She glanced back at him and gave a slight shrug. "I finished my education in a private high school and a women's college back east. Then I came back to the Bay Area and spent a few years as a so-so cub reporter for the *San Francisco Chronicle*. Fifteen years ago I joined the staff at *Youngest Sister* magazine."

Shane rested his elbows on his knees and propped his chin on his fists, smiling. "And there you still are, Miss Merry, writing an advice column for young girls in love."

"I didn't think you'd know about that," she said, half-embarrassed.

"Oh, I know lots of things." He got up to stand beside her. "You're still Merle Pierce . . . you're not married?"

"I was, but it didn't work out." She wrapped her arms over her ribs, as if protecting the unhealed wound. "I took my maiden name back."

"So you're a free agent." Speculation gleamed in his blue eyes.

Flustered, she lifted her arms and smoothed wisps of pale hair back from her face.

He seemed very big, almost overwhelming, beside her. She took a couple of steps away. "Now it's your turn to fill me in. What have you done with your life since . . ." She flipped her hand.

Shane stared at the storm clouds massing beyond the western hills, over the unseen ocean. "After I got my leg put back together, I came home and threw Pop and the boys into shock by taking up law. They had me earmarked to be a cop like them."

She smiled. "Why did you decide to become a lawyer?"

He shrugged. "I suppose I liked the ring of it."

"It must have been a loud clanging ring, judging by how often you turn up in the news."

He glanced at her out of the corners of his eyes. "You've been following my career, have you?"

"It's impossible not to, when you do things like leading a small army of teenage prostitutes up the steps of City Hall on Christmas Eve. The police looked like storm troopers harassing children after you got through with them. What on earth were you trying to prove?"

"It's the publicity I'm after, Merry."

She rubbed her neck. "I don't know how you can do it. The thought of having my name smeared all over the papers gives me the creeps. I treasure my privacy too much."

His face lit up with a grin, his eyes hot, his chin raised. "Oh, it's kind of fun, like a game. But the end result is serious. A lot of those kids come from abusive homes, and if they're picked up, they're more often than not sent back to be abused. I'm lobbying in my own humble way to have anonymous safe houses set up, where my runaways can get counseling and job training."

"Humble!" She laughed, then sobered. "But you can't tell me your activities don't put a strain on your personal life. Are you married?" She held her breath for the answer, though she told herself it made not an iota of difference in her life.

"I tried it once. No children, simple divorce." He shrugged again, holding his shoulders up for a few beats before letting them down. "I live on a houseboat in Sausalito."

She studied his face, wondering what made him tick. "It sounds as though you lead an interesting and unusual life."

"Mostly it's frustrating and lonely." He seemed uneasy talking about his personal life. "Your hillside is covered, so I suppose I'd better go."

"I suppose." Merle climbed the hill, part of the way on all fours where the slope was slippery, with Shane following by the same mode. She watched silently as he washed his hands under the faucet outside her house and wiped them on his jeans, then put on his leather jacket.

Stepping forward, he brushed a smear of mud off her cheek with a fingertip. "Do you suppose it would work for us to see each other again?" It was a casual, careful question. "You and me."

Her entire body came alive with an ache for him. The temptation was strong. But once around with Shane Halloran was enough for any woman. She shook her head and smiled apologetically to take the sting out. "We don't have much in common. You're such a daredevil and a rabble-rouser, and I'm so cautious, my assistant calls me prissy. I'd be afraid for my career if it came out about you and Ellen, and—" She broke off when she began to sound prudish.

He narrowed his eyes. "Are you trying to say Ellen and I and my connection with the girls I represent might dirty your reputation, *Miss Merry?*"

The tone of his voice, and the fact that she'd almost said just that, irritated her. She jutted her dimpled chin out. "And exactly what's wrong with Miss Merry?"

Shoving his hands into his pockets, he rocked back on his boot heels. "I've read 'Ask Miss Merry' from time to time. And you're right, you aren't exactly a radical."

"Miss Merry fills a valid need. My girls are sincerely concerned about things such as kissing and sex. But I don't suppose you can understand something so simple, considering."

He made fists of his hands in his pockets. "Probably not, when my girls are sincerely concerned about attracting the next trick so they can earn enough money to eat."

"That doesn't mean my girls' problems aren't just as important!" she said, her voice icy. "If I can talk one of them out of getting into the situation I got into with you, then I'll consider myself a success."

Shane stared at her with smoldering eyes, two vertical lines cutting between his brows. "If that was a left-handed attempt to blame me for your getting pregnant with Ellen, then let me say you were just as hot for me as I was for you. Why didn't you use contraceptives?"

"*I* should have used contraceptives? *Me?!*" she sputtered. "That's exactly the mentality that makes Miss Merry so important to naive young girls!" She looked him up and down. "I warn them away from guys like you."

Somewhat belatedly, she wondered what had induced her to say such hurtful things. It wasn't like her at all.

Shane looked at her for several seconds. "I guess I'll have to agree with you—we couldn't make a go of it." Jaws knotting, he clamped his teeth shut.

After a few moments he gave a rueful smile and stepped forward to brush her forehead with his lips. "But it's been interesting seeing you again, Merry."

Lifting her hand to touch the tingle left on her skin by his kiss, she gave a regretful smile. "Yes . . . yes, it has been that, Shane."

After he'd fired up his motorcycle, Merele stood by the corner of the house, watching him sway and weave down her steep driveway. He picked up speed on the access road along the freeway. Suddenly she gasped and threw out both arms as if somehow she could stop him from accelerating up the on-ramp into a collision course with a pickup truck. "*Shane, be careful!*" she screamed, though he couldn't possibly hear. She went limp with relief when he zipped into the lane, missing the truck by a hair.

Then she burst into tears because seeing him had brought back too many hurts and had stirred up desires she'd never thought she'd feel again.

The near collision left Shane shaken and prickling with cold sweat. He wasn't ordinarily a reckless driver; past experience with trauma had left him phobic of doctors and hospitals, consequently leery of accidents.

But he wasn't thinking straight. His mind was too full of Merry, his body too full of wanting her. If that was true, why had he fought with her? *Why?*

He needed to talk, and there was only one place he felt comfortable doing that. Ten minutes later he parked the cycle in front of his twin sister Bren's house in Berkeley.

A big grin lit her face when she opened the door. "Well, hello, stranger," she cried out. She was tall and rangy in jeans and a blouse. Shane noticed the silver in her hair had mysteriously turned black again. "Come on in. Dan's working, and the kids are Lord knows where, so we can talk in peace and quiet."

He took off his muddy boots by the door and followed her into the kitchen to sit at the table. She sat down opposite him. "So what's the problem? The only time you come around is when you need to talk."

Shane rubbed his palm against the left side of his blue T-shirt and told her about Ellen, ending up with, "What's she like? Let's just say she might be surprised by the Halloran side of her biological background."

His twin laughed. "Most people would be. Is that your problem, the family?"

"No. The problem is I went to see Merry today and found out I'm still so upset about stuff that happened when I was eighteen that all I did was pick fights with her. I told her she should have used contraceptives." He jabbed himself on the chest. "Me, the man who based his entire life on human rights, I said that. I'm telling you, I reverted to a raving adolescent."

Bren got up and lit the flame under the teakettle. "I never could figure out what you saw in Merle Pierce. She was always so proper and . . . anemic."

Shane jerked himself upright in the chair. "She was not anemic! People didn't notice what a beautiful girl she was because she had a quiet exterior, but inside she was . . ." He couldn't think of a way to explain how it'd been with Merry. She'd responded to him with an explosive sensuality that had rocked him.

"You remember how I was in the sixties, don't you? Everything was flower children, make love not war, down with the establishment. And me so embarrassed to think my father was a street cop—one of the pigs." He held up two fingers a quarter inch apart. "I came this close to sinking into the drug and sex scene. The only reason I'm halfway normal today is because proper little Merry snapped me back into sanity."

"Okay, I give up. She's wonderful." Bren poured boiling water on coffee crystals in two mugs.

He scowled. "Damm it! I'd as soon jump between the jaws of a great white shark than have Merry find out how badly she hurt me."

"Then if I were you, I'd stay away from her. That'll be two bits for my advice."

"I didn't ask for any," Shane said grumpily.

"Here's another piece of advice, whether you want it or not. Forget that your brothers and sister have produced a dozen perfectly fine grandchildren. Mom and Pop are heartsick over not having one from you. They'll never forgive you if you don't tell them about this daughter of yours."

He groaned. "Why in hell does life have to be so complicated, Bren?"

"Because you attract complications like a dog attracts fleas, that's why."

Two

Dear Miss Merry,
There's this boy at school in the next row over. And I don't know why, but something inside me really wants him. You know— wants *him. Is what I feel love? Should I try to get him to go out with me even though he's a jerk?*

Wondering

Dear Wondering,
What you are feeling, my sweet, is the hormones in your body responding to the hormones in his body. This is lust. True love is being attracted to the personality of a very special boy, as well as feeling a sexual attraction. My advice is to stay away from this boy. Don't waste yourself on a less than perfect love.

Miss Merry

Merle glanced at her watch for the third time in as many minutes. Then she fidgeted in her desk chair, staring at her computer screen. She'd been good for nothing ever since Ellen had called to arrange another meeting. Her work, which had been her lifeblood, had sunk far down on her list of priorities in the ten days since she'd met Ellen. Thoughts of her daughter had taken over her entire mind. Well, most of it—Shane kept niggling his way into her thoughts whenever she let her guard down.

She jumped an inch when a voice over her shoulder said, "Don't you think lust and hormones might be a little daring for our new editor in chief? What's her name—I can't remember." Her assistant, Louise Miller, had swiveled around from the other desk in the small office to scan Merle's computer screen, reading her answer to Wondering.

"Do you really think so?" Merle sat up straight and reread the letter.

"*I* don't, but—" Louise picked an interoffice communiqué out of the pile of clutter on Merle's desk and held it up. "Avis Simmons, that's her name. Ms. Simmons Legree might think so. This is the fourth memo she's sent you in three weeks about that sort of thing."

Merle snatched the memo and crumpled it up. "How, in this day and age, can she suggest my advice is too worldly and graphic for the early teen range of my readers?"

"Maybe she and the new owners of *Youngest Sister* think the pendulum is swinging away from the sexual revolution."

"You don't suppose they're just scratching around for an excuse to phase me out, do you?"

"I wish I could answer no to that."

Merle got up and paced restlessly, looking at the pictures and school photos wallpapering her office. For fifteen years she'd transmitted her unfulfilled maternal love to her young fans via Miss Merry. And they'd returned it tenfold. How desolate her life would have been without them.

Sighing, she stopped to stare out her sixth-floor

window. The second storm in three days had passed without dropping much rain, and now the weather had cleared. The ocean was a glittering turquoise under the late afternoon sun. A fog bank hunched on the far side of the Golden Gate Bridge was threatening to pounce on the City. Sausalito and Shane's houseboat were up the bay somewhere, north of the bridge. The thought of him brought Merle's brows down over her eyes. So he thought she wasn't very radical, did he? What gall. Who did he think he was?

"I refuse to water down my advice. My girls need to hear about sexual responsibility." Stalking back to her desk, Merle defiantly saved her answer to Wondering's letter as it was and turned off her computer.

That done, she glanced at her watch and felt her heart jump. It was time. She closed the door of the office and took out a makeup mirror. As she fixed her face, she examined herself critically. Never mind her elegant bone structure and dramatic coloring, all she saw were parentheses bracketing her nicely bowed lips, and cheeks that had lost the roundness of youth. Squinting caused fine wrinkles to fan out from her large brown eyes. "I need emergency plastic surgery," she said despondently. "I look like a hag."

Louise reached over Merle's shoulder to flip the mirror around. "Who doesn't, looking at themselves with magnification? Where are you going, anyway?"

"Ellen asked me to have dinner with her this evening and meet her fiancé. I'm so thrilled. I was afraid I'd never see her again." Merle grinned jubilantly, then frowned and added, "Shane will be there too."

Louise gave her the eye. "You aren't still in love with him, are you?"

"How ridiculous! All we do is fight." Merle put away her mirror and makeup, then added wryly, "Though there may be a teeny bit of Wondering's lust involved." She smoothed the ecru wool dress down over her hips.

"With Ms. Legree breathing down your neck, I'd say lusting after a man as notorious as Shane Halloran could mean trouble with a capital T," Louise said, her brow cocked.

"Then I'd better take my own advice, hadn't I?" Merle said, waving an airy hand at her monitor. "But not to worry, everything is under control. When it comes to Shane, I've got enough emotional shields up around myself to protect the starship Enterprise," she said as she checked the amber jewelry at her neck and ears, then slipped into a brown coat.

Within the hour she was in an Italian restaurant on Fisherman's Wharf, weaving her way around tables with checkered cloths in a crowded dining room.

The other three people in her party were already at a table in the rear. Ellen jumped up and rushed forward. "I'm so glad you could come," she said, then put her arms around Merle and kissed her cheek.

Merle gathered her daughter close for a second, as she'd been yearning to do. "Love, I would have mowed down anyone who got in my way," she whispered. The pesky tears that always seemed just beneath her surface threatened to well up again. She blinked them away when Ellen drew back. They both turned toward the men.

Shane was lounging back in his chair with an impish grin on his face. He drew Merle's gaze like a magnet, which really wasn't surprising, considering that his chinos had holes in the knees and his tweed jacket was hopelessly wrinkled. The logo in his moth-eaten yellow T-shirt declared, The Homeless Do It in the Open, and his running shoes were air-conditioned at the toes. She resisted an urge to make an acid comment; she'd decided for her daughter's sake not to let the explosiveness their last meeting had produced happen again.

Ellen's face shone with love and pride as she pulled her fiancé forward by the hand. Rob Taylor was a tall, slim young man in a suit and tie, with brown hair in a stylish cut. His handshake was warm, his smile genuine, and Merle decided he was perfect for her daughter. After they'd exchanged formalities, Ellen gestured back to the table and announced, "Shane's here too."

Merle looked him over with a cocked eye as he came forward. Incredibly he looked sexy and urbane even in his appalling outfit. "I couldn't help but notice—he isn't likely to fade into the woodwork, is he?" she said.

A grin spread over Shane's face, and he brushed at his jacket. "These are my streetwalking clothes. I've been trying to make contact with some new girls in town, and they try to pick me up if I look too affluent. Sorry, I didn't have time to change." He didn't sound a bit apologetic.

Merle studied him curiously as she unbuttoned her coat. "Most men would be tempted by all those available young girls."

Shane stepped behind her to slip his fingers under the collar of her coat, bending his head close to murmur in her ear. "I'm not tempted by children, Merry. My problem is resisting a real woman."

She shivered at the sensation of his fingers against the curve of her neck, and stepped quickly forward, leaving her coat in his hands. "Well, try really, really hard."

His eyes sparkled. "You're being prissy again, Miss Merry."

"And you're trying to start a tiff, but I'm not biting."

"A tiff is the farthest thing from my mind, believe me." Shane folded her coat on a chair and seated her at the table.

The others sat down too. Ellen very seriously assumed the role of hostess. "As you see, we already have our drinks. What would you like, Merle?"

"Nothing. I'm content to sit here and enjoy being with you and Rob and—" She glanced at Shane. Flickering candlelight glinted on the silver in his black hair. His gaze traced her lips, probed her dimpled chin, touched on the full breasts pressing up under the supple wool of her dress. Shields up, she reminded herself. "Well, I'm not so sure about you," she said, scowling to fight off a smile.

Eyes sultry and aware, he pushed out a pouty lip and lifted his glass of mineral water in a salute.

Ellen looked quizzically at them, misinterpreting their bantering for animosity. "I suppose I shouldn't have invited you both at the same time, but I knew you'd talked . . . and ages and ages have passed since you . . ." She ran a hand over her smooth, dark hair, realizing she was wading in deep water. Then she jumped in with both feet. "Well, I just thought all that sex stuff wouldn't bother you anymore at your age."

Shane glanced at Merle, his eyes widening. He rubbed his hand over his mouth to wipe away a laugh. Turning to Ellen, he said in a terrible fake brogue, "Girl, heart o' mine, there may be some gray hairs on my head, but my memory ain't gone yet. I'm still bothered by sex stuff, oh, maybe once or twice a year. I'd venture a guess that Merry might be too."

Merle didn't want to laugh when Ellen looked so serious. She grabbed her water glass, then went into a spasm of choking when a swallow met a giggle in the middle of her throat. That set Shane off into a shout of laughter.

"What's so funny?" Ellen demanded, mystified.

Rob grinned. "I think you've put your foot in your mouth, sweetheart."

"Why? What did I say?"

Shane patted her hand. "Did I forget to tell you foot-in-mouth disease is a genetic defect running in my side of your background? I'm blessed with the problem myself, too often. Right, Merry?"

"Right, Shane."

The conversation throughout dinner and dessert was animated, friendly, and well seasoned with laughter. Shane's flirtatious little byplay continued, and though Merle tried valiantly, she wasn't quite able to hold herself aloof. Her gaze insisted upon wandering back to meet his.

Even Ellen loosened up as they debated their views on everything from families to politics. She sighed happily as they were lingering over coffee. "I didn't realize I'd like you so much. I wonder . . . would it be appropriate for me to ask you both to come to my wedding and sit on my side of the church? Sort of take my parents' place, since they . . . can't be there." A worried look pinched her face as she glanced from one to the other.

Tears blurred Merle's eyes. She reached out and squeezed her daughter's hand. "Darling Ellen, I'm absolutely delighted that you want me at your most special occasion."

Shane lifted Ellen's other hand to his lips. His eyes were suspiciously shiny too. "I don't give a damn whether it's appropriate or not, darlin'. I'll be there with bells on."

"I'm so glad!" Ellen said, then retrieved her hands and checked her watch. "Oh, gosh, I didn't realize it was so late. I have to be in the lab by six in the morning, so I'd better go home and get some sleep." She jumped up and enfolded Merle, then Shane, in a hug. Seconds later she swept Rob away in a flurry of good-byes.

Merle lingered outside with Shane, listening to the soft romantic music lilting from the restaurant behind them. It was pleasant on the wharf, the air ripe with the scent of the restless, slapping waves of the bay. The sky was very dark, only the brightest stars visible over the glow of streetlights. A big moon was hanging low over the shops.

She was much too aware of Shane's tall body next to hers for comfort. A tremor ran down her spine, ınd she pulled her coat close, as if the action might ward him off or protect her from herself—or both. She knew she should leave, but she didn't take the irst step away from him.

Shane had his hands in his pockets, jingling change and shifting from foot to foot. It occurred to ıer briefly that he was acting like a bashful boy, but she knew he was too much a man of the world for hat to be possible.

After a bit he said, "Merry, I want to apologize for ighting with you last Saturday." His eyes were warm ınd sincerely apologetic. "I don't know why I said vhat I did, I don't even believe half of that trash. It vas as if a demon got into me."

She gave a laugh and clasped her hands in front of ıer chest. "I'm glad you brought the subject up. It vasn't just you, I said a quite a few things I wish I ıadn't too. It's beyond understanding how two maure, educated, intelligent adults could have regressed into such childish bickering. I'll accept your ıpology if you'll accept mine."

"Deal." They were silent for a few moments, as if outting off the moment of parting.

"It was fun being with those two tonight, wasn't t?" Shane finally said.

"Oh, yes. It seems like a dream or a gift to have Ellen come back into my life."

"Ditto here. I've always kind of missed being a ather. I can't help thinking about all the years of her ife we lost. She's so serious and such a controller, I vonder what she might have been like if we'd orought her up?"

"I've wondered that too." A deep sense of regret over he loss of her child—and of him—swelled up in her chest. The stirring of those buried emotions prompted her to say good night. "I'd better go home ıow."

"Where's your car parked? I'll walk you to it."

Merle pushed her purse strap up on her shoulder

and wrapped her arms around herself. "That's generous offer, seeing as it's parked twenty or s miles away in Lafayette."

"How are you planning to get home, then?"

"I'll ride the cable car downtown and take BART th rest of the way."

"I'll give you a ride home."

Merle glanced sidelong at him. Night shadows ha blackened his hair and made smudges of his eyes giving his face a mysterious aura. After the way she' been responding to him all evening, she'd be a fool t go off alone with him. "Thanks, Shane, but I'm use to getting around by myself," she said firmly, an began walking toward the well-lit cable car stop a fe blocks away.

He grabbed her arm and stopped her. "Good Lord woman, you can't run all over San Francisco at night You'll get mugged or worse. Let me take you home!

She jerked her arm free. "Good Lord, man, the wa you drive that motorcycle of yours, I'd be safer wit the muggers."

He made a sheepish face. "I suppose you saw th trick I pulled getting on the freeway last Saturday?

She nodded slowly, remembering how his reckless ness had frightened her.

"Well, I don't always drive like that. Besides, I've go my car tonight."

"Thanks, but I'd rather not." Merle began walkin toward the lights again, hugging her purse for com fort.

Shane fell in step beside her. "You won't ride wit me, because you haven't forgiven me for the fight, i that it?"

She walked faster, her heels clicking on the side walk. "I forgave you, but that doesn't mean I want t be buddies."

"Did I say anything about buddies? Did I? All I'n doing is offering you a simple ride home."

"Oh, sure. And what about the goo-goo eyes you were making in the restaurant?"

"What goo-goo eyes?" He kicked a pebble, sending it skittering down the sidewalk. "So what if I happened to be doing a little flirting? I certainly couldn't tell by your reaction that it was insulting to you. In fact I could have sworn you were receptive."

That he was so close to the truth was too much for her to accept. "Good grief, Shane, will you go home! I've been taking perfectly adequate care of myself without you for twenty-three years!"

Suddenly she realized her voice had risen. Stopping short, she threw out her hands, then grabbed her purse when it slid off her shoulder. "Will you listen to me! We've only been alone together fifteen minutes, and we're at each other already."

Shane stopped, chin up, looking surprised. "We are, aren't we? And I only just got done apologizing for the last time."

Merle brushed her hair back from her face. "I guess this tells us what would have happened if we'd brought Ellen up. We probably would have fought from day one and ruined her life."

He opened his mouth, then closed it again and grinned. "My first impulse was to argue it wouldn't have happened, but I suppose that'd defeat my point."

Merle gave a laugh. "All right, walk me to the cable car stop. I might even admit the idea of walking alone scared me. I was just being perverse."

"Okay, then I'll admit I wasn't so much worried about you as that I wanted to be with you for a little while longer."

"See how impossible we are?" She began walking slowly, her flared coat skirt swaying around her slender legs.

He ambled along beside her, his limp adding a jazzy rhythm to his walk. His knees canted out to the sides, showing skin through the frayed holes in his chinos as he took one long-legged step to each two of her high-heeled ones. He was so big and vital; it confused her to feel physically safe with him and yet so emotionally insecure.

The cable car stop was the end of the line. The crowd of tourists in the turnaround were encapsulated in the circle of light from the street lamp, with the salty smell of the ocean and the dark of night pressing against their backs. A young street musician was playing an achingly beautiful love song on a guitar, with his instrument case open on the sidewalk for donations.

Standing beyond the outer fringes of the tourists, Merle focused her entire consciousness on the man beside her.

After a few moments Shane poked the holey toe of his running shoe at a gum wrapper on the ground. "I've been thinking about our bickering. It could develop into a problem, you know."

Merle smiled sadly up at him. "I doubt that we'll be seeing enough of each other to worry about it. We don't exactly travel in the same circles."

"But we'll be coming into contact with each other for Ellen's wedding festivities. Do you suppose we can get along for that?"

Her smile wavered. "Oh. I'd forgotten about that."

"I don't imagine she'd like us to be hissing and spitting at each other like cats while she's walking down the aisle."

"For once I agree with you," she said thoughtfully. "We haven't done much else for Ellen, so it seems the least we can do now is act friendly and help make her wedding special."

"I can't argue with that." He grinned, his eyes teasing. "See how well we're doing? I do believe we'll be able to manage a truce, at least up to and through the nuptials. Care to seal it with a handshake?" He held out his hand.

Merle stared at it, suspicious of what he thought

was involved in a truce. After a moment's hesitation she nodded grudgingly and offered her small hand to be swallowed up in his large one. His callused palm stimulated the soft skin of hers so that a melting sensation rushed through the rest of her body, centering at her core. The twitch at the corners of his lips told her he was aware of her reaction. She jerked her hand back and rubbed it against her coat.

Heart racing, she quickly turned away to stare at the guitarist, scarcely hearing his music. She breathed a silent prayer of thanksgiving when the cable car pulled up with the screech of wheels on iron rails.

After the passengers had poured off, the gripman hand-pushed the antique car onto the platform and around in a circle until it was heading back toward town. When he gave the signal, the waiting crowd surged forward. Shane bullied his way through, clearing a path for Merle, and handed her up onto one of the outer benches.

Within seconds every inch of space inside and outside the car was jammed. The gripman released the brake and dinged his bell. Shane held onto a bar and took a few steps along as the car jerked forward. "Want me to ride with you?"

Merle smiled, dimples dancing at the corners of her mouth, and reached between two people to pat his cheek. "No thanks, love, we aren't safe together."

The two fascinated people obligingly made room when he stepped up onto the ledge, his lopsided grin lighting up his face. "Darlin', would you be sayin' this truce of ours might be a trial by fire?"

"That's exactly what I'm saying, and I hate getting my fingers singed."

"Well now, that sounds promising."

She shook her head so firmly that wavy white-gold hair whipped around her cheeks. "Only in your wildest fantasies."

He laughed, his sultry blue eyes speaking volumes,

and then he stepped back off the car onto the street and signaled thumbs up.

Merle felt a teary sense of emptiness when the car lurched forward and labored up to the top of the first steep hill, leaving him behind. She recognized the empty feeling as a warning not to be foolhardy. It would be dangerous to take the attraction between her and Shane lightly.

If only . . . , she thought, then shook her head again. Nothing could possibly come of it—they were poles apart in every aspect. The safest route was to make certain they didn't end up alone together again. Luckily there wasn't any reason for her to see Shane until the wedding, which was over four months away.

But despite her wise judgment, the notion didn't sit easily, and her heart sank right along with her stomach as the cable car plummeted down the other side of the hill.

Three

Dear Miss Merry,

I'm fourteen, and me and my boyfriend like to talk in privacy in my room with the door shut. We don't plan to go any further than a kiss, but my mom acts like we're holding an orgy. How can I convince her I can control myself?

Misunderstood

Dear Misunderstood,

At fourteen a woman's libido is still new to her, love. You don't understand how overpowering sexuality can be. An innocent kiss can touch off so strong a desire for intercourse that your controls may be blown away. My dear, I must advise you to explore your love in public with the doors open and people around.

Miss Merry

Dozens of letters from adolescents came in every day. Merle and Louise shared the responsibility of writing the replies. Misunderstood was one of

Merle's. She ripped the letter off the printer and put it in the self-addressed envelope. "I wonder if little Miss Misunderstood will take my advice? They're always so sure they know everything at that age."

Louise gave a short laugh. "You said intercourse, that's daring enough to catch her attention." She held out a small white bag. "Want a cinnamon drop?"

Merle dipped her hand in and popped one in her mouth. Swiveling her chair toward the window, she slipped off her pumps and leaned back to gaze lazily out at the view. Gulls were gliding over the bay, wheeling and yawing gracefully. The afternoon sun was shining on shore, but the perpetual cottony fog bank was lying in wait just beyond the bridge.

As happened too often, despite her shields, Shane came to mind. Merle idly rolled the cinnamon drop around her mouth with her tongue, trying to figure out why he affected her so strongly. He was attractive, no doubt about that. Most men had the grace to enter middle age with a potbelly and a bald head, but not Shane. Still, she'd dated men who were more handsome, a couple of them considerably younger, but they hadn't sent her libido into a tailspin.

Curling her tongue around the candy, she drifted into a series of vague thoughts, wondering about his day-to-day life. Did he date many women—naturally he did, he wasn't the type of man to live a monastic life. It didn't sit well to picture him with other women. She fantasized herself in the picture instead.

The telephone rang; she cradled the receiver against her neck and said dreamily, "Merle Pierce speaking."

"Hullo, Miss Merry Pierce." Shane's voice lent a soft sense of presence to her mental ramblings.

She jerked upright and inhaled her cinnamon drop, gagging as it went down her throat.

"You all right?"

"I'm fine. Just fine," she said, fanning her face. "I didn't expect it to be you, that's all."

"Oh, is that all? Well then." He sounded as if he had his feet up on his desk.

She couldn't handle any more imagery concerning Shane. Slipping into her shoes, she aligned her chair with her desk and straightened her skirt. "What can I do for you?"

"I need to talk to you."

"Here I am, all ears."

"I'm not the telephone type, I need to see a person's face so I can read her expression when I talk—must be the lawyer in me. Can we meet someplace?" When she didn't answer immediately, he said, "It's important, there's something concerning Ellen I need your advice about. Actually I need your okay."

"My advice and my okay?" Curiosity overcame her reservations. "Where do you want to meet?"

"I thought we might have dinner."

"Shane!"

"Don't get in a stew. No ulterior motives, I promise. Remember our truce."

"No dinner."

"Okay, should I come up to your office?"

"*No!*" Merle could picture the stir he'd cause if he turned up on the premises of *Youngest Sister*. "Maybe we could have coffee somewhere. I just finished what I was doing, so I'm free now."

"Good. Meet me at Riley's Place a few blocks down the street from your building in a half hour. Okay?"

"Okay." She hung up and took her mirror out of a desk drawer.

Louise watched with high interest as she freshened her makeup. "You have a dewy-eyed look. You sure something isn't starting up between you two again?"

Merle pinned her pale hair up into a pouf on top of her head, with tendrils around her face. "Nothing's starting. I know Shane for exactly what he is."

After slipping on her jacket, she looked irritably down at her navy blue suit and tugged at the neckline of her white blouse. "I wish I'd change my style, I always look so *blah!* Like a . . . a spinster."

Louise gave an exaggerated sigh and took a brightly flowered scarf and a pair of dangly earrings out of her bottom desk drawer. Merle draped the scarf over her shoulder and slipped the earrings into her pierced ears, then nodded with satisfaction at her image in the mirror. "Thanks," she said, and rushed out of the office.

She speedwalked the two blocks from her office building to Riley's Place, arriving only ten minutes later.

Shane was waiting outside. She almost didn't recognize him in a charcoal-gray suit and vest over a white shirt and a maroon tie, a briefcase under his arm. Suddenly he wasn't the man she was so certain she knew. There was a command and power about him that she hadn't noticed before.

He grinned when she walked up, and reached out to flip a dangly earring with his finger. "You look pretty spiffy."

She backed out of range. "Thanks, you look pretty spiffy yourself. I didn't think you owned anything but T-shirts and jeans."

"I had to dress to impress for an important meeting today." He brushed an imaginary bit of lint off his sleeve, then held the door of the pub open with an extended arm, briefcase in his hand. "Now that we've taken care of the mutual admiration, should we go in?"

Merle walked past him, catching a whiff of his musky male scent and citrus cologne. She clutched her purse more tightly, imagining she felt a magnetic pull drawing her toward him.

He looked down at her and sniffed. "You smell like cinnamon—makes me want to taste you. What kind of perfume is that?"

She laughed. "It's a secret formula."

The Irish pub had a bar and brass railing across one end, dividing the bar area from the dining section where booths with high backs were tucked along the paneled walls. Even early in the afternoon there was a crowd of working-class clientele and tourists, drinking dark beer and listening to raucous live Irish music.

Riley, the owner, greeted Shane as if he were a long-lost friend, slapping him on the back and singing out, "Well, if it ain't Pat Halloran's boy! We haven't seen you here in a month o' Sundays. What have you been gettin' yourself up to, me boy?"

Shane patted the top of his own head. "I've been getting myself up to about six-two, Riley."

"Ahh, ain't you the quickwitted one?" Riley led them to the far corner, out of the noise and hubbub. "This here's me own private booth. Will that do?" He fussed around. "Can I bring you a pitcher of beer now, or some grog?"

Shane lifted his brows at Merle. "How about it?"

She shook her head. "I never developed a taste for the stuff. But you go ahead."

"Too early in the day for me. Riley makes a pretty mean brew of tea. How about that?"

At her nod, Riley brought a steaming pot, two china cups and saucers, a plate of scones, and declared it on the house. When he left, Merle let out the laugh she'd been biting back. "How do you happen to know him? Is he an import from County Cork?"

Shane grinned. "Riley's accent is cornier than corned beef and cabbage. His parents came to California in the gold-rush days with my grandparents, so he's like family. Pop and the boys think this place is great." He peered at her. "If you hate it, we can go somewhere else."

"No, I love it. It's wonderful." She picked up her cup and sipped. The tea was Earl Gray.

Shane sugared his tea and stirred it. "Did you ever meet my family? I can't remember."

"A few times." She glanced up at him, little snippets of memory rising from the great store she had worked so hard to bury and forget. "All I remember is your house exploding with loud talk and strong personalities. I was used to being an only child in a quiet, proper family, so they scared me to death."

A grin lit his face. "You probably reacted that way because of what you'd been doing with their son."

Half-angry and half-embarrassed, Merle blushed.

Shane jerked at his tie as if it'd been choking him and unbuttoned the top button of his shirt. "Speaking of my family, that's why I wanted to talk to you." He scratched his cheek. "I know you didn't want our past broadcast, but I had to tell my parents about Ellen. They aren't the kind of people you can keep a granddaughter a secret from."

Merle cringed, wondering what they thought of her. "How did they react?"

His eyes sparkled. "If I'd been eighteen, they would have boxed my ears for what I did to you, but there isn't much they can do now." He leaned his elbows on the table, braced his spoon upright in his teacup with a fingertip, and looked at her anxiously. "They want to meet Ellen, but I put them off. Is it okay with you?"

"Oh . . . I don't know what to say. I hadn't thought about it going any further than you and me." Eyes lowered, she listened to the Irish band rasp and twiddle above shouts of laughter from the pub patrons. "I can't picture our methodical Ellen and your family together. Still, I know she's very lonely since her . . . parents died." She glanced up at him. "It's really not my decision to make, it's Ellen's. Why don't you ask her what she wants to do?"

Shane touched her hand with a fingertip. "You're really a nice, unselfish woman, Merry, you know that?"

She felt a rush of warmth. "So are you, a nice, unselfish man. It was considerate of you to ask me how I felt before going ahead with it."

Shane's smile softened as he saw the open acceptance on her face. He traced the shape of her lips and the curve of her cheek with his eyes, then captured her gaze with his.

Frightened suddenly, Merle looked down, only to become enthralled by the sight of his parted lips. She touched the tip of her tongue to her own lips, wanting his kiss. Wanting him.

It took force of will to tear her gaze away, and her hand was shaking when she lifted her cup to moisten her dry mouth with tea. The cup clattered when she put it on the saucer. Logic told her their business was finished and it was time to go; an inner ache pleaded with her to stay with him. She shifted her feet but couldn't bring herself to rise. Just a few minutes couldn't do any harm. Fifteen at the most, then she'd leave.

Breaking a scone to busy her hands, she initiated a neutral topic for conversation: "You said you're dressed to impress for an important meeting. I thought all you did was represent down-and-out girls."

Her question roused Shane from some inner struggle of his own. Drawing in a deep sigh, he shifted position and leaned forward on his elbows with his chin on his fists. "Remember my best friend in high school, Barney Krenshaw? I'm in law practice with him and his father and their group. Luckily they support my cause and give me lots of freedom."

"I vaguely remember. Is there anything I can ask about the case you're on?"

He smiled. "Ask any damned thing you want. My current client and I told all to the reporters at a press conference just an hour or so ago. I'm representing a young woman who's suing her stepfather for physically and psychologically abusing her when she was a child." He grinned and gave the briefcase on the bench beside him a self-satisfied pat. "It's a dream case made in heaven for a man of my interests."

Merle sat up straight, scowling. "How can you be so glib about something as awful as child abuse?"

A flash of anger lit his eyes. "Oh, come on, Miss Merry, lots of awful things go on in this world, and I've seen my share on the streets. Sighing and moaning doesn't help. The only way to accomplish anything is to stand up and make yourself heard."

She gave an apologetic smile. "Sorry, you're right, of course. And you've more than demonstrated your concern over the years." She leaned forward, elbows on the table, chin on the heel of her hand. "Tell me about this girl."

"She ran away at age fifteen to escape the abuse, and walked the streets, hooking for a year or so. But she was smart and gutsy enough to stay away from drugs and claw her way up out of the gutter. She's been supporting herself very nicely since, though I doubt Miss Merry would approve."

Merle stared at him, running the possibilities through her mind. "I'm afraid to ask, but how *does* she support herself?"

"Well . . . she didn't have a high school diploma, but until age fifteen she'd been reared in an upper-class family to be a beautiful, poised, articulate woman—the perfect assets to become a high-priced call girl."

She lifted her chin off her hand, her back going rigid. "Surely you don't think being a call girl is a step up! How disgustingly chauvinistic!"

His brows came down defensively. "It's a hell of a lot safer than working the street! I'm not saying it's every mother's dream for their daughter. All I know is she's struggling to rise above her background. She's putting herself through college on what she earns in the evening. That's how she got smart enough to realize she's a piper who ought to be paid for her lost childhood."

The reality of that poor girl's life began to sink in, and Merle nodded slowly. "Yes, I understand."

"And I intend to do my best to see that the people who failed her are held accountable." His eyes were alive, his face strong, his voice aggressive.

She smiled slightly. "She's lucky to have you for her lawyer—with that look on your face, you can probably convince a jury of anything."

He gave a snort of laughter. "Only time will tell."

He lifted both hands, palms up, and made a face. "If you don't stuff that last scone down my throat and shut me up, I'm likely to be off and running all afternoon—bore you to death."

Merle leaned forward. "I'm not bored, I'm fascinated by what you do."

A pleased grin crept over his face. "That's sweet of you, but now it's your turn. What else do you do besides write a monthly column?"

She lifted her hands to touch the heavy, pale gold roll of hair on top of her head, her dark eyes thoughtful. "I don't do anything even remotely as exciting as your legal shenanigans. I answer the letters coming in from the girls and choose the ones we run. I travel quite a bit giving talks about sexuality at girls' clubs and schools all around the country. In fact, I'm leaving on a month-long speaking tour in a week or so. I keep saying I'm going to write a book about growing up for my teenyboppers, but I never seem to get around to it."

Shane listened with his head cocked, his eyes intent on her face. "Teenyboppers?"

She smiled affectionately. "My teenyboppers are young female persons who need to learn how to fight for the dignity and human rights you advocate. I teach them to expect only the very best out of life, and that no one has the right to use or abuse them. As happened to your client."

"Good." First he smiled, then he made a face. "I shouldn't have sneered at Miss Merry that first day. I only did it because you'd turned me down and my feelings were hurt. Where'd you come up with all your wisdom?"

Merle brushed a few scone crumbs into a pile on the table, then glanced up at him. "It's fairly easy to relate to my girls when I can still distinctly remember how it felt to be a confused, troubled teenager myself."

Shane nodded, his face sympathetic and regretful. "Those were bad times." For a few minutes he listened to an Irish ballad being played. Then he looked at Merle. "What about when you aren't working? Are there men in your life? Is there anyone special?"

"I know a few men, and sometimes we see each other. No one special. How about you and women?"

"Same as you, there are a few women I go around with sometimes, but no one stands out."

She searched his face and found an empathy that encouraged confidences. "I haven't had much luck hanging on to the men I've cared about."

"Did you love your husband a lot?"

"I guess so, I think so. Not as much as—" She almost said, "as much as I loved you," but faltered to a safer finish. "I didn't love him as much as I should have. That's probably why our marriage failed. Though it seemed as if it ended because I couldn't get pregnant."

Shane had been looking down, playing with his cup, now he glanced up. "I didn't realize you couldn't have children. That must have been a kick in the teeth after what happened with Ellen."

"Yes, you could say that." Merle watched his tanned fingers circle his cup. "My husband and I went to an infertility clinic but didn't have any luck with the simple solutions. He didn't want to get involved in anything as complicated as in vitro fertilization or the like. Then he got another woman pregnant—

while we were still trying. They had their baby right after our divorce was final. I still hate him a little bit for that."

Shane's gaze moved over her face—gently, not seductively. "I think I hate him, too, sight unseen." His expression enfolded her with sympathy. "Why didn't you get married again and do in vitro with a new husband?"

Merle glanced wistfully at his broad shoulders, at the pulse in his throat, the broad chest under his vest. "I don't know . . . I ended up leery of romantic involvements. It's been eight years, and I'm still scared I might get hurt again."

He nodded his understanding. "Did you ever think about going for an in vitro and single parenthood?"

"I know single parenting is all the rage now, but I'm old-fashioned enough to think a baby needs a traditional family, with a mother and a father and stability." Then she decided she'd said all she cared to about her infertility, and cocked a brow at him. "Why? Are you making some kind of kinky proposition or something? Are you interested in donating sperm, or what?"

His lopsided grin spread over his face. "Nope. If any sperm of mine ever find a home, you can be damned sure I'd follow through and love the result."

She looked at him a second longer, touched, and allowed herself to consider the possibility. Then she shook her head firmly. "No, it's too late for me to be a mother. Even if I approved of single parenting, I'm too old to bear children. If by some miracle I happened to get pregnant, I'd have to worry about something being wrong with the baby." She smiled then. "But I am a mother in a way. My teenyboppers are the children I never had."

He nodded. "I guess I feel fatherly toward the girls I work with too. Though they're enough to drive a parent to drink."

They were quiet for a time, listening to the music.

Then Shane spoke. "I've got a bit of the same problem as you about involvement. I ended up feeling beaten and bloody when my marriage didn't work out. Even when I knew it was my fault."

Merle leaned forward and supported her chin on laced fingers, gazing at him. "I'm sure it wasn't all your fault."

"No, this time it was my doing. My wife went all out to make it work. I gave her lots of *things*, a beautiful house in the Oakland hills, an unlimited charge account, but I couldn't love her the way she wanted to be loved. It was as if my heart was locked up tight and I couldn't find the key."

Shane lifted his cup and made a face over a stale cold sip of tea, then replaced the cup carefully and precisely on the saucer. "I did a lot of soul-searching after that, and I finally figured out there's something missing in me. I'm not sure I'm capable of a marriage kind of love. Does that sound ridiculous?"

She curled her fingers around his wrist. "Oh, no Shane, it sounds sad. It makes me want to cry."

"So, now you know why I'm leary of permanent relationships. It isn't fair to offer a woman half a loaf. You were wise in backing off from me. I'm bad news." He fitted his other hand over hers on his wrist.

A bond seemed to be circling around the two of them, flowing out of the connection of their hands and their shared regrets. It frightened her a little. She pulled her hand free and quickly filled the silence with a question. "Didn't you tell me before that you live on a houseboat in Sausalito? That must be quite different from living in the Oakland hills."

Shane grinned. "Have you ever seen a houseboat?"

"No, I haven't," she admitted, shaking her head. "Tell me about it."

"It looks a little like a . . ." He stared off into space for a moment, then shook his head. "A description can't do it justice. Would you like to see for yourself?" He lifted his brows. "I'd be proud to show it to you."

The bond that had grown between them was such that Merle didn't even hesitate. "I'd love to see it."

"Wonderful!" Shane got up and picked up his briefcase, offering his other hand to her. "Come on then."

She pulled back out of reach. "I'm not riding on that motorcycle of yours."

"If you're going to be hard-nosed about it, I suppose we can take the ferry over."

"That sounds like fun." Merle put her hand in Shane's and blithely walked out of the pub with him.

Four

Dear Miss Merry,

My mother says boys are nothing but animals and all they want from a girl is sex. Is that true? When I'm out on a date, sometimes I feel like all I want is sex from my boyfriend. Does that mean I'm an animal or unnatural?

Worried

Dear Worried,

My sweet, boys are people, the same as you and me. Sexual appetite is normal in all human beings, girls as well as boys. The difference between animals and humans, love, is that a girl or a boy can simply say no to desire until the time is right.

Miss Merry

Merle held on to the railing with both hands, bracing herself against the rise and dip of the ferry as it breasted waves. A stiff, pungent ocean breeze snatched at her scarf and suit skirt. Shane was standing beside her, so close that her shoulder brushed his upper arm; her heartbeat was vibrating, thrum, thrum, through her veins, mimicking the thrum, thrum of engines under the deck.

The fog bank had advanced until only the towering pinnacles of the Golden Gate Bridge were poking up out of the thick wall of white. Within minutes the ferry had plowed into the veil. Fog enfolded Shane and Merle, separating them from the few other passengers riding on deck.

"It's eerie," she said, her voice hushed.

He nodded. "Like an alien world."

The mournful hooting of foghorns and the lonely cries of unseen gulls sent a shiver up her spine.

"Are you cold?" Shane asked, looking down at her. "Would you like to go inside and sit in the cabin?"

"No, it's not that cold. I feel like a kid on an amusement park ride, and I don't want to miss anything."

He put his briefcase down on the deck and held his gray suit jacket open. "How about sharing body heat?"

Logic advised caution. But what could happen in the middle of the day on board a ship? And she *was* chilly, after all. "Good idea," she said, fitting her back against his front.

Her head fit perfectly into the curve of his neck. She could hear the strong, quick beating of his heart. He closed his arms around her, crossing them just under her breasts. It was as if she'd always known the feeling of his long, muscular body against hers. She felt such a peaceful sense of coming home that she drew a huge sigh up from the bottom of her lungs.

Shane sighed simultaneously. "I love a woman who isn't afraid to risk a little cold for an interesting experience," he murmured, moving his chin against the softness of her wavy hair. "Not that I'd put riding a ferry on top of that list."

"It is to me. I'm ashamed to admit that after all

these years I've lived in the Bay Area, I've never ridden a ferry before."

"What's even more shameful is that you have but you've forgotten." The breath of his words felt warm to her scalp. "Angel Island is right over there to the right of the bow. Surely you remember that."

Peering over the bow at the limited circle of restless waves enclosed by the white wall, she resisted remembering, afraid of the feelings that would come along with the memory. "There isn't anything there but fog."

"Trust me, it's there."

"When was I at Angel Island? And why do you have such a good memory of what I have or haven't done?"

"Oh, come on, you can't tell me you don't remember the day we ditched school and rode the ferry out there together." He pulled the jacket a little closer, cuddling her against his body. "It was in April, I think, not long before I graduated from high school. My friend Barney worked up a reasonable facsimile of your mother's handwriting and wrote a sick excuse for you the next day. Surely your remember *that*."

"Well, maybe I do remember," she admitted, a smile playing around her lips. "But what would my teenyboppers think if they found out Miss Merry lied to play hooky?"

Shane's voice was husky. "They'd think, hey, Miss Merry is a real person. She's had some heavy decisions to make, too, and didn't always make the wise choice. They'd say, we can believe in Miss Merry, she knows where it's at."

Merle hummed skeptically. "Bet their parents wouldn't agree."

"What they don't know won't hurt 'em." He laughed softly. "I take it you're beginning to remember the day."

"I remember enough to wonder how I could've forgotten. Must be a quirk of the subconscious, protecting me from my checkered past." She turned her head and smiled up at him.

The creases dimpling his cheeks and fanning out from his eyes deepened with his expansive grin. "Devilish device, the subconscious—covers up anything that might make you blush."

A gust of salty wind blew his suit collar up on the back of his neck and flattened his silver-black curls over his brow.

Merle leaned the back of her head against his chest and looked out into the fog. Now that she'd surrendered herself to this tiny slice of the past, she could picture exactly how he'd looked on the ferry all those years ago. His body had been lanky and revving with energy. She smiled at the memory. "Back then your hair was so frizzy and stood so far out around your head that you looked like a wild man."

"Yeah, well, yours was a yard long, and you used to iron it on the ironing board to straighten the wave out."

She laughed, nodding. "It's hard to believe I ever did anything that dumb. If I remember correctly, back then everyone wanted to look like John Lennon of the Beatles, kind of pasty with granny glasses. I looked that way naturally. I wonder what you saw in me."

"I thought you were the most beautiful girl in school, Merry," he said softly. "And the odd part is that you're lovelier now than you were as a girl."

"Shane, what an outrageous statement!" she exclaimed, pleasure radiating inside her. "I think you've picked up your father's Irish blarney."

"No blarney, just telling it like it is. I remember you as being round in the face and maybe a little too straight and bony in the body as a girl, not that I minded. Now you're all curvy and graceful, and your face is . . . oh, I don't know how to explain it . . . full of fascinating planes and mysterious angles. You could be a model, I bet."

"Far be it from me to disillusion you." She changed a subject that was becoming too personal and too current. "Do you remember how you tried to walk tightrope on the railing, and the captain bawled you out? He practically threw you off on the island. And then we—" She broke the sentence off when the full memory returned.

Shane laughed mischievously; she could hear the rumble in his chest behind her ears. "Didn't we just! I can see us yet, sneaking into forbidden territory, running and bounding like two crazy people down a gully between two hills. Nobody around but a herd of deer."

Merle laughed. "We were wearing those awful hip-hugging, bell-bottom jeans with the huge stringy holes in the knees, and matching T-shirts."

"Uh-huh." His chin brushed her hair when he nodded. "And we both stripped buck naked and threw 'em to the wind."

"Oh, my Lord!" Merle exclaimed. "Was I *ever* that uninhibited?" Oddly, she didn't feel the slightest embarrassment, even while standing in the circle of the same man's arms, talking about it. A sense of sadness crept over her. "Why does the innocence of youth have to disappear? I could never bring myself to do anything like that now—throwing off my clothes outdoors."

"It's not the innocence that disappears," Shane said, pulling in his stomach behind her. "It's the skin tone that sags. At forty-one I'd think several times before running nude in front of someone I wanted to impress."

Merle burst out laughing. "There is that factor to consider, yes. You have a wonderful way of putting things into perspective."

They fell silent then. She preferred to touch back on the rest of the outing privately, and apparently Shane felt the same. She saw them standing in the sun surrounded by brush and tall grass. They were laughing with the pure joy of being themselves, in love and together, with the sound of the waves crashing on the shore, the smell of wildflowers. They'd shouted at the tops of their lungs, setting the herd of deer off in terrified flight. Then they'd made love hidden by a screen of nature.

Usually their lovemaking had been forbidden and frantic, but that one day had been theirs. They'd had hours of time to explore every inch of each other's body. It all came back to her—the silky skin of Shane's shoulders, the muscles in his arms and chest standing out like a relief map, the coarse hair on his legs and chest and around the staff of sex he'd offered her.

Merle suddenly became acutely aware of the same body against her back, of Shane's breathless stillness, his erection against her buttocks. She was filled with aching desire. She wanted him now. She stirred, ready to turn around and claim his lips, to hold him in her arms. But if she ever kissed him, she'd be lost.

Wrapping her fingers around his solid wrist, she pulled his arms loose. Stepping away from him was difficult. At the railing she couldn't stop herself from glancing wistfully up at him.

His eyes were molten blue lava. His lips were moist and parted. He put a world of questioning need into the murmuring of her name: "Merry . . . ?"

Wind tore at her hair; she welcomed its chill on her hot skin. Words of refusal didn't come easily. She dredged up a thick voice to say, "We'd better let the past lie slumbering where it's safe, Shane. With our track record, it'd be a disaster if we let anything start up again."

The lines across his forehead deepened, as if he were torn. He rubbed his face with both hands and ran his fingers through his hair, and then he asked, "How do you know it would, unless we give ourselves a chance?"

"I just know, that's all. I can feel it in my bones." Merle turned to stare out over the bow. "I shouldn't have come on the ferry with you."

Shane leaned on the railing beside her and glanced at her, grinning a challenge. "If you're worried about stirring up the past, you probably shouldn't have."

"Well, I'm sure we should be able to control ourselves for an hour or so, shouldn't we?" she said pointedly.

Each time the boat surged up on a wave, his shoulder brushed hers, nurturing the smoldering spark of desire. One part of her mind warned that she was playing with fire; in another part of her mind the simile struck her as funny and made her laugh. Consequently she didn't pull away from his touch as she knew she should.

Sausalito was very close now. The yearning moan of the foghorns and the siren call of the gulls seemed to pull them forward.

After disembarking, they walked in silence along the pier toward Shane's houseboat, Merle maintaining a prim distance. The embracing blanket of fog picked up every sound like a microphone. Metal clanged against metal, wood grated against wood, a subdued word, a laugh, the slap of waves, mysterious whispers and moans, the beads on Merle's dangly earrings jingling.

The houseboat wasn't what she'd expected. It was solid and permanently moored, and its deck resembled a minuscule, picket-fenced yard with potted trees and flowers, deck chairs and table. The door was painted dark red to brighten the white siding on the flat-roofed house, the effect eerily softened by mist. "It doesn't look a bit bizarre," she said, surprised. "I didn't expect anything so conservative, knowing you."

"Maybe you don't know me as well as you think you

do." Shane opened the door and stood aside to let her enter first.

She hesitated, looking up at him with narrowed eyes. "No passes."

"No passes, I promise." He grinned and crossed his heart with a finger. "You're safe."

"I better be, I've got enough complications in my life without . . ." She gave him a final warning look and walked into his private, personal space.

He closed the door, shutting out what little world the fog hadn't already obliterated. It was as if they were the only two people left on the planet. She turned, tempted to retreat while she still could. She knew instinctively she could trust him. But herself . . . ?

Shane's irresistible, proud smile kept her there. "This is it, my place. Go on in and look around."

Taking a deep breath and maintaining a firm grip on her safety shields, Merle looked around the combination living room–dining room–kitchen. Her first impression was that it was handsome, comfortable, welcoming, very neat, with a clean masculine scent—just like the man himself. "It doesn't look like a boat," she said with interest.

"Sure it does." He threw his briefcase down on a chair and flipped switches to light up brass wall fixtures and a crystal teardrop chandelier, then pointed out brass railings mounted at both sides of each door, wood wainscoting, dark blue brocade draperies, and a captain's wheel. "I got all these things off a retired luxury liner by sheer luck. That's why I bought the houseboat, so I'd have a place to put them."

The rest of the furnishings were almost stark to balance the ornate fixtures: a contemporary sofa in light blue, a red easy chair, a lemon yellow one, Scandinavian dining and occasional tables. But Merle was more mesmerized by the easy, loose-hipped way Shane walked, the rhythm of his limp, and his expansive hand gestures than his tales of decorating woes.

He tugged at his tie. "A little bit of this dress-for-success business goes a long way. Would it be construed as a pass if I took off my tie and jacket?"

She shook her head. "I don't suppose so."

He slipped his jacket and vest off and folded them over the back of a chair. His trousers were beltless and fit his hips like a second skin. He took off his tie and unbuttoned his shirt down three buttons, giving breathing space to the fluff of black hair on his chest, then he rolled up his shirtsleeves to the middle of his forearms. It may not have been a pass, but Merle saw his simple divesting of outer garments as more sexy than a male strip show she'd once seen.

"Why don't you take your jacket off too and make yourself comfortable?" She jumped, startled by the sound of his voice.

"No, I'm fine." She drew the colorful scarf more securely around her shoulders and wandered about restlessly, looking at paintings and out the window, inspecting the gleaming ceramic tile and bronze appliances in the kitchen.

"Do you want a drink? Wine, or something stronger? Or weaker?" Shane offered, his male scent curling around her in invisible tendrils. "Are you hungry? It's getting late. How about I make dinner?"

"Oh, no, I'm not staying long enough for any of that." She fumbled for an excuse to leave while she still could. "I need to . . . I've got to . . . to catch the ferry back before it quits running for the night."

He looked down at her, his lips curved in a slight, knowing smile. "I *could* drive you home, you know," he said softly in his smooth, deep voice. "Then you'd have time to have dinner here."

"No, thanks." She took two sensible steps toward the door.

He spoke quickly. "I'm a pretty good cook, if that's scaring you away."

She stopped and looked back at him. "I'm sure you are, but I don't think it's the best idea for me to be here with you. In fact I'm certain it isn't."

"Why?" he asked, a grin twitching the corners of his lips. When he pushed his hands into his pockets, they added an interesting stretch across the front of his trousers.

Merle felt giddy suddenly and jerked her gaze away from his fly. "You know perfectly well why, Shane Halloran. I've got to go."

"But you haven't seen the rest of my place yet. It'll only take a minute, and I'm really interested in hearing what you think about it."

Merle glanced sidelong at him, vacillating. He did look sincere, and, true to his promise, he hadn't made an actual pass. He hadn't so much as touched her. "All right, show me the rest. Lead on."

Shane led the way, pointing out all the amenities. Down the hall was a bathroom, compact and gleaming. In a guest bedroom across from the bathroom were twin beds with pale yellow comforters. Merle mouthed proper, admiring comments.

"Last room on the hallway is the master bedroom," Shane said, his voice low and very detached. "My bedroom." He stood aside for her to enter.

It seemed oddly warm in the houseboat. Merle's face flushed with heat, though her skin was puckered in goose bumps. Standing well back from the door, she glanced into the large bedroom. The first and only thing she saw was the bed. The royal blue spread had concentric circles of primary colors radiating from the edges to the center. The image of a target leaped to mind. An arrow hitting the small circle at the center.

That was it, all she could tolerate. Whirling around, she crashed into Shane, who stood directly behind her, and threw out her arms for balance. He threw out his arms to catch her. Their arms closed automatically around each other.

"Sorry," he said, his voice husky, his lips against her hair. "You okay?"

"No, I'm not!" she cried out. Her face was pressed against his chest, and her nose was buried in the puff of black hair at the base of his throat. His heart thundered under her ear. Every nerve in her body had come alive. The spark of desire ignited while they were on the ferry burst into flame, and desperate need fueled her motions.

Throwing her arms around his neck, she pulled his mouth down to hers. He met her lips with bruising intensity. There was nothing tentative about the way he kissed her, open-mouthed to demand entry into once-beloved territory. She moaned deep in her throat when he probed her mouth with his darting tongue. She moved fluttering hands over his shoulders and his neck, ran her fingers into his crisp, curly hair.

"This isn't a pass, Merry, I didn't . . ." His lips moved over her face, fanning the fire inside her body to incandescent heat. "I'll quit . . . in just a second."

"Yes, we've . . . got to stop." Her skin burned under her clothes as she moved her pelvis against the swell of his desire. He opened his thighs, his arms crushing her lower body against his.

Lifting his head, he looked into her face with tortured eyes. "Oh, Lord, I'm sorry, Merry, I shouldn't have—"

"No, no, we can't—" Pulling away from him, her fingers trembling, she ripped open the top button on his shirt, and the next, then the rest of them.

Her jacket fell to the floor, and he fumbled with the button and zipper of her skirt, finally sliding it down over her hips and thighs. "Merry, my Merry, are you sure you want this?"

"No, no. . . ." She pulled his shirt off his arms,

kissing the wonderful pelt of hair on his chest, his nipples.

"Do you want me to stop?" he asked softly, unbuttoning her blouse, fingers caressing her full breasts.

"No, no. . . ." Opening her arms, Merle helped him remove her blouse. "Oh, hurry, Shane. I need you."

It was too slow, too frustrating. They separated to throw off their own clothes, each watching the other with smoldering eyes. Whimpering with impatience, she jerked her slip over her head, feeling his gaze on her body as he hopped on one leg to strip off his socks. He unzipped his trousers, then stopped, lips parted, to watch her peel down pantyhose and panties at once and kick them off her feet.

"Wait," he whispered when she reached in back for her bra snap. Stepping forward, his face flushed, his eyes glittering, he cupped a palm under each breast in its silken restraint and bent forward to kiss the swell of flesh, wetting her skin with his tongue. Then he reached behind and undid the catch, slipped the straps slowly down over her shoulders. After the bra fell, he cradled her breasts and took each of her aching nipples in his mouth.

She cried out as the sensation shot through her body to her core. "Hurry, Shane, *hurry*."

Pushing down his unzipped pants and shorts, she took his sex into her hands, stroking the satiny, tight skin. She cried out with pleasure when he pulled her against his body. "Now, Shane, now."

"Yes, Merry, oh, yes, now. I've wanted you for so long. Let me come home to you, my love, my only one." Bending his knees, he slid into her and straightened, his hands under her thighs lifting her up against his body. Leaning on the wall to support their combined weight, he began to move inside her.

Clutching his shoulders with her arms, Merle

threw back her head and moaned when he began the rhythm she'd known so long ago.

"My Merry, I love you." His voice rose with urgency, a little louder with each pump, getting faster, stronger, deeper. "Merry, Merry, Merry."

"Oh Shane! Oh Shane, IloveyouShane," she cried out. Contractions vibrated through her body. Just when her climax was ending, he echoed her release, spasming against her. Finally his head fell back against the wall.

Merle buried her face in the curve of his neck and burst out crying. Her gushing tears mixed with the sweat of his shoulder as she sobbed like a child.

Shane snapped his head forward. "What's wrong, Merry? Oh, Lord, I'm sorry. I didn't mean to hurt you." He began to let her slide down his body.

She tightened her arms around his neck and wrapped her legs around his hips, clinging to him. "Don't . . . oh, hold me, Shane. I'm crying . . . because it's . . . been so long." Her words were punctuated with sobs. "It's never been . . . I've never felt like this with . . . anyone else. I've missed you so. Just hold me. Hold me."

Back pressed against the wall, he held her against his moist body with gentle arms, moving his lips against her hair, her brow, her ears, whispering, "You eclipse the moon, the sun, the universe, my Merry."

She gave a long, shuddery sigh. "We're awfully good together—at least this way."

His cheek was pressed against her forehead, she could feel it move with his grin. "Even slam, bam, like this?"

Merle laughed, actually giggled, then lifted her head to look into his face. "This *is* a little ridiculous for people of our age."

"Awesome, yes, but not one iota ridiculous." Shane let go of her with one arm to wipe the tears off her lashes with his fingertips.

She tightened her legs around his hips and her arms around his shoulders. "I must look terrible." She hid her face against his neck again.

Shane lifted her chin with his fingers. "You look more beautiful to me right now than you've ever looked in your life, Merry." The expression on his face made it the truth.

She sighed happily. "You know what's so amazing about this?" she said after a moment.

He smiled. "Everything, but go ahead and tell me what amazes you."

"It isn't like me to jump at a man the way I did at you. In fact there have been times when I thought I might be a little . . . well . . . frigid."

"*You*?" Shane laughed. "You almost singed my eyebrows."

She laughed too. "That's what I mean, I went insane the instant you touched me. How odd that I don't feel one bit strange or shy with you."

He nodded. "It's not odd; we broke each other in a long time ago." Then he drew in a quick breath. "Speaking of long ago, with our history you'd think I would have remembered to use a contraceptive. Oh, Merry, I'm sorry. Everything went so fast—I didn't think."

"I can't get pregnant, remember?" Unwrapping her legs, she slid down to stand within the circle of his arms.

He brushed his lips against her hair again, thinking for a few moments. "If I ever fantasized about making love to you since we were kids—not admitting whether I have or haven't, mind you—I would have at least had us in the bed."

She laughed. "No, it really wouldn't do a thing for your reputation, love, if it got out that you grabbed a lady and had your way with her in the hall."

He laughed too. "You're the one worried about your reputation, not me. And as you pointed out a minute ago, I wasn't the one who did the grabbing—you jumped my bones."

His hands were moving down her back now, cupping her buttocks. She shivered slightly and kissed his nipples until she felt him stiffen again.

"Quibbling aside," he whispered, his breath coming quickly, "I really think we ought to rectify our lapse and check out my bed, don't you?"

"Oh, yes." She felt a delicious floating sensation when he picked her up and carried her to his bed.

This time they took each other gently and slowly, amid teasing and laughing and words of love. Later they lay quietly in the big bed, a sheet over their damp, sated bodies, legs entwined, arms around each other.

"There's never been anyone like you in all the years we've been parted, darlin'. I feel as if I've just been given my life back again." Shane's deep sigh lifted her head on his chest.

She sighed too. "Mmm-hmm, it's as if I've been wound up too tight all these years, and suddenly I'm sprung." She played her fingers slowly through his chest hair. "But I have a deep, philosophical question for you. How come your hair is going silver on your head, while it's still black on your body?"

He lifted his head to look down at his chest, then dropped it on the pillow again. "I dunno, maybe because my brain is so powerful, it's frying the color out."

"Oh, brother, talk about humility." She tweaked a chest curl.

He grabbed her hand and smiled. "This proves one thing, anyway."

"What's that?" She curved her palm around his rounded bicep muscle.

"The truce worked. We're not fighting."

"I'm so limp, I couldn't fight to save my neck."

He circled his fingers around her throat. "You won't have to, I'd save your neck anytime it's in danger."

Merle reached under the sheet. "How? You're limper than I am."

"Don't get personal, darlin', you might send me into a mid-life crisis."

She laughed. "Male menopause is bound to whiz right past a man with your level of humility."

Shane laughed too. After a bit he sighed contentedly. "This is awfully nice, isn't it?"

"Uh-huh."

"Merry? Wouldn't it be something if we could make things work between us?"

She studied the jut of his nose, the sensual curve of his lips, the character lines that broadcast the passionate, flamboyant nature of the man. "It'd be something, all right," she said wistfully.

He looked up into her face, at her gentle eyes, her sensitive lips. "It'd be a shame if we lost each other again, wouldn't it?"

She thought about it from every angle. "What did you have in mind, Shane? I'm not keen on having some kind of an affair."

"I don't know. But it'd be sad if we let ourselves drift apart without seeing if we could build something solid."

"I'll have to think about it." She wrinkled her brow for a second. "Okay, I've thought. The conclusion is I'm hungry, starving! You can cook me that dinner now."

"Sorry, I can't move." He flopped his arm out on the bed and closed his eyes. Then he went into a spasm and jerked his knees up when she tickled him on the stomach. "You're a hard woman, Miss Merry."

"No, I'm not. To prove it I'll let you take a shower first."

Grumbling good-naturedly, he threw back the sheet and got out of bed. Merle's smile died as she watched him limp out into the hallway to collect his clothes. Now that the fever pitch of their lovemaking was over, she saw the terrible scars on his right leg.

The extent of the damage jolted her heart, and she wanted to ask him about it, to comfort him now, so many years later. But he seemed self-conscious about his leg and slipped his trousers on before coming back through the bedroom to go into the master bath. She suspected he wouldn't appreciate her pointing it out.

In five minutes he came out of the bathroom barefooted and headed for the kitchen with his shirt hanging unbuttoned. Merle hopped into and out of the shower and put her skirt and white blouse back on, leaving the top buttons undone. She slipped into her heels without pantyhose, put on lipstick, and tied her wet hair back with the flowered scarf.

Out in the living room, she put her purse and jacket on a chair by the door and went into Shane's arms when he came out of the kitchen.

"You look lovely, darlin'," he said, smiling down at her. "Like a freshly scrubbed little girl, all pink and rosy from being kissed and loved." He bent his head and added a little more redness to her lips.

They both jumped when a crisp knock sounded on the door.

He groaned. "Who the devil could that be? I wanted to think we were the only two people in the world." Reluctantly releasing Merle, he turned to yank open the door.

She was standing just to the left of and behind him when several flashbulbs went off, blinding her and sending her into horrified shock.

"Oh, cripes! Not now, not yet!" Shane whispered harshly, his hands tightening into fists.

The young man heading up the group of several reporters stepped forward. "Mr. Halloran, Fenton Hollbrook has answered your news conference by saying your case for the call girl is a heap of garbage. He says he'll clear himself of abuse charges if it takes his last dollar. And he's got millions. Would you care to comment?"

Shane turned his body to shield Merle from view. "I am so sorry about this, Merry," he whispered. "We'd better get you out of here before they figure out who you are."

He grabbed her purse and jacket off the chair and pushed them into her hands, then took her elbow and steered her through the door, plowing the group back and shielding her from view as much as possible. Merle ran off the houseboat, wanting desperately to be gone, to run away and hide.

Everything seemed to be working against her. Even the concealing fog had thinned, and she had to run down the pier almost a block before she was hidden from sight. She reached the landing, only to see the ferry still far out on the bay, just emerging from the fog. The biting wind sent shivers through her body and set her teeth to chattering. Or maybe she was shivering because her feelings were so confused and stormy, she thought.

Staring miserably at five synchronized pelicans gliding past, she berated fate. How, when she had found such excitement and tenderness in sharing physical love with Shane, could something so inane as a troup of reporters come along to shatter the magic? But why blame fate? The man attracted that sort of fiasco like a magnet.

Logic told her it hadn't been his fault—it was her own. She'd lived such a careful life since the last time she'd gotten caught up in a black comedy with him. So *why* had she been with him this afternoon? It was ridiculous for a mature woman of almost forty to go gaga over a man and end up in such a situation.

Sighing deeply, she acknowledged the lesson learned from the experience: If she wanted peace of mind, she had to stay away from Shane. As it was, the best she could hope for was that the reporters wouldn't use the picture with her in it. And if they did, that no one would recognize her. It wasn't too much to ask. Was it?

She jumped when the ferry, forging toward the landing, gave a derisive hoot, almost as if answering her question.

Five

Dear Miss Merry,
I had my school pictures taken last Monday. Wouldn't you know I woke up that morning with two zits, one on my nose and one on my chin! Why do things like zits pick the worst possible time to happen?

Ruined

Dear Ruined,
My darling, of course you aren't ruined. I'm sure you're a lovely girl in your picture. As to why—when your body is getting used to a powerful new set of hormones, stress, such as worry over a picture, can bring on blemishes. I must smilingly refer you to Murphy's Law, which says, If anything can *go wrong, it will.*

Miss Merry

It was raining again the next day when Merle left the office and took a cab to meet Ellen at a bridal shop. She wore dark glasses and a hat pulled low.

Ellen came running up late and joined her under

the canopy in front of the shop. "Sorry about the short notice, but when they called to say my dress had come in, I wanted to see it right away. It seemed sad to see it by myself, so I took a chance that you might want to share the excitement."

Merle hugged her daughter close and kissed her cheek. "Love, I would have gotten out of my deathbed to see you in your wedding gown."

A sassy sparkle gleamed in Ellen's eyes as she drew back. "You didn't appear anywhere near your deathbed in this morning's paper."

Merle groaned; things were really bad when even her somber daughter was inspired to tease. "I was so hoping you wouldn't have seen that."

Ellen took a *San Francisco Chronicle* clipping out of her purse and waved it under Merle's nose. "Oh, I always read the paper first thing. And how could I miss my two favorite people, right on the front page?"

The headlines in big bold letters declared, ACTIVIST AND CALL GIRL GO UP AGAINST FENTON HOLLBROOK. The picture under it hadn't changed since Merle had first cringed over it. A disheveled Shane was at center stage, and there she was right behind him, looking equally disheveled.

"What I can't understand," Ellen said, frowning, "is how they mistook you, of all people, for a call girl."

Merle gasped in horror; the possibility hadn't occurred to her. "*Not me!* They mean the woman Shane's representing!"

"Oh. I guess the picture combined with the headline is somewhat misleading."

Muttering something under her breath that it was just as well Ellen didn't hear, Merle whipped off her sunglasses and shoved them in her purse. "I feel as if I'm living in a nightmare! I can't imagine what my boss is going to do when she sees the picture. Things can't get any worse."

Ellen laughed. "Things can always get worse. So let's go see my dress, okay?"

A few minutes later Merle was sitting on a spindly velvet-and-gilt chair watching a couple of attendants smooth and pat an ivory satin gown over Ellen's tall, willowy body. She looked regal in the swooping train, long pointed sleeves, and pearl-encrusted bodice with a deep V neckline.

After the buttons on the back and sleeves had been fastened with a hook, one of the attendants stood back. "Well, Mother, what do you think of your little girl now?" she asked Merle.

Merle's heart gave a yearning, wishful jump, but then she looked quickly at Ellen in the mirror, hoping she hadn't taken offense out of respect for the adoptive "real" mother she'd loved so dearly.

But instead a pleased, tender look warmed Ellen's face. "Yes, what do you think, *Mother*," she asked softly, linking gazes with Merle. "No, 'Mother' seems too formal for you." Shane's impish smile blossomed on her face; she was in a rare mood today. "Mum? How do I look, Mummy?"

Tears rose in Merle's eyes. She smiled tremulously, her voice catching as she said softly, "I think my little girl looks just like a princess."

While the attendants fussed around Ellen, measuring for alterations, Merle watched, suffused with joy. It didn't matter that Ellen had made the first step toward a mother-daughter relationship with all the flippancy of youth. The great inner emptiness Merle had felt for twenty-three years was starting to be filled.

Then her smile faded into an introspective frown. If she'd finally become a mother, it seemed just about time to stop floundering into messes and take charge of her life.

Which meant she had to come to some understanding of the impossible situation sprouting up like a weed between her and Shane. To her acute distress, she hadn't been able to stop thinking about him—all through the long restless night. He'd tried to phone the previous evening and that morning, but her answering machine had interceded at home and Louise had done the same at the office.

What she felt for him seemed almost like love, but that couldn't be—they had absolutely nothing in common. Hadn't she thought she was in love with him before? And look at the agony she'd gone through. She'd done the same thing with her ex-husband; what she'd felt for him had been different, not as intense, but she'd thought it was the real thing. Wasn't she always telling her girls that lust could masquerade as love for a while? Everyone with any maturity knew that.

So, if she couldn't trust herself to recognize true love, she'd be a fool to set herself up for pain by jumping into a whirlwind affair and have it backfire on her. Hadn't she just cited Murphy's Law to a teenybopper in one of her columns? That was reason enough to steer far clear of Shane.

The problem was that her entire system resisted the idea of giving him up again. Heaven help her—he'd made her feel young and alive and sexy again. Probably for the first time since she'd been sixteen.

Merle gazed at Ellen's fresh, youthful face in the mirror, and then at her own mature face. No matter how Shane made her feel, she wasn't a kid any longer. Far from it. It was time to begin acting her age.

Shane sat at the table in his twin sister's kitchen, scowling at the front page of the *Chronicle*, suffering the tortures of the damned. He and Merle had barely begun to know each other again. Things were fragile and tentative between them yet—and the damned picture had probably blown everything apart.

"I don't know what to do, Bren," he said, looking up with haggard eyes. "If only I could talk to Merry and explain. I've tried calling her at home and couldn't get past her answering machine. I've called her office a dozen times this morning, and supposedly she's either in a meeting or out. I think she doesn't want to talk to me."

"Well, can you blame her?" Bren cocked an eye at the picture. "But if she won't talk to you, Mom and Pop will. They've already called me, thinking I might know why you were so witless as to drag Merle into a press conference with your feet bare and your shirt-tail hanging out. What were you guys doing, any-way?" Her smile was knowing.

"None of your damn business." He jumped when his pager beeped, and stumped across the kitchen to use the phone. After hanging up, he turned around, his face a mask of surprise. "Merry made an appoint-ment to meet me at my office in an hour. I wonder if she's bringing a forty-five to blow my head off."

"If you weren't my beloved twin brother, I'd say you deserve it."

He curled his lip at her. "I suppose it ought to be some consolation to know things can't possibly get worse."

"Any mother can tell you—things can always get worse." Bren grinned. "But it'd help if you could once learn to keep your pants zipped."

It took Shane longer than he expected to fight the traffic, stow the cycle in the parking garage, and wait for the elevator up to his office. He barely had time to run an electric razor over his beard, flatten the curl of his hair with the palms of his hands, and rub the tops of his boots on the backs of his jean legs before his secretary buzzed. "Ms. Pierce to see you."

"Send her in and hold my calls."

Nervousness had made him hot, so he took off his leather jacket, then looked down at his red T-shirt and muttered, "Oh, cripes!" The logo read, Legal

Stud. He barely had time to scramble back into his jacket before Merry walked in.

She was holding herself stiff and formal in a gray suit with a short jacket over a pale blue blouse. But he could see the beautiful woman behind the professional facade. The crystals in her ears winked rainbow colors through the tendrils of pale gold hair escaping from the twist on her head. Her brows and lashes made a dark contrast to her peach-blossom skin. "Hullo, Merry," he said, stepping forward to test the atmosphere.

She backed away, warding him off with her hands up. "Oh no you don't, Shane. I'm not tempting fate a second time," she said, her dark eyes flashing. "Why didn't you warn me you were going after Fenton Hollbrook before you dragged me off to your houseboat? Good grief, the man's an institution in San Francisco society and one of the wealthiest financiers in California. That's like going up against a *god*. Naturally the press would be hounding you. How *could* you plop me into the middle of something like that?"

Her tirade was so close to an accusation that the demon inside him awoke, despite his better intentions. "I didn't pick you up and plop you in the middle of anything. You came with me willingly enough."

She crossed her arms. "But you knew the reporters would be after you for a statement."

His eyes narrowed. "Are you suggesting I used you for a publicity ploy? If you think that, then what the hell are you doing here?"

"Believe me, I thoroughly scouted out the territory before I risked it. But you *did* know, didn't you? Go ahead, admit it."

"All right! Yes, I knew, dammit! But—" He broke off abruptly, coming to his senses. He started over again in a reasonable voice. "Merry, I swear I didn't get you into this mess on purpose."

Her shoulders drooped. "*Why* did this have to

occur just when something beautiful had happened between us? I feel so—" She bit her lip.

Shane's heart swelled with love for her and with regret that things never seemed easy for them. "Ah, Merry, darlin', I'm sorry. I didn't think the press would find me so soon. I didn't even realize they knew where I lived."

She sighed deeply, lifting her full breasts under her suit jacket. "Oh, it isn't your fault, Shane. I know that. It's mine, because people who live in glass houses shouldn't let themselves get into compromising positions."

He didn't like the sound of that, and studied her face, searching for some shred of hope. "About the picture . . . has anyone recognized you?"

She gave a humorless laugh. "You mean other than Louise, Ellen, and anyone else who knows me at all? Luckily I'm leaving town in a few days on that speaking tour of mine, and I'll be gone a month. If I accept a few more engagements, I can stretch it out to six weeks or even two months, and maybe everything will have blown over before I get back."

"Maybe." He was pretty sure it wouldn't, but he didn't care to go into that. Probably it was fortunate she'd be gone, but the thought made him feel lonely.

Merle sat down on the chair in front of his desk, put her purse down, and crossed her slender legs. "Believe it or not, I honestly didn't come here to fight," she said with a wry smile.

Shane perched on the corner of the desk and braced a pen between his forefingers, searching her face. "Why *did* you come, Merry?"

"I've been thinking a lot about the consequences that might arise from the picture. I need you to tell me more about this lawsuit of yours, just in case someone recognizes me and asks me what I think. I wouldn't want to sound any more stupid than I already look."

Slipping the pen over his ear, he clasped his hands

around his knee and rocked back on the desk. "What do you want to know?"

"Everything, anything you can tell me."

Shane outlined the case for her, ending with: "The last incident of abuse before Linda ran away involved a laceration requiring several stitches, which was explained away to the hospital and doctors as the result of a fall."

Merle's eyes flashed with anger. "The man is a monster! And her mother, her family, and her schools turned blind eyes to her helplessness? They're all guilty! They all forced that poor child out onto the streets to peddle her body. But Hollbrook, he deserves to—" she lifted her hands, searching for the words, "to have the *book* thrown at him."

Shane smiled at her old-fashioned cliché, then rubbed the back of his neck. "Justice is fickle, Merry. I just found out a very prestigious firm is standing up for the man, which means I'm nothing but a kid lawyer playing way out of my league. Hollbrook is apt to get off without so much as a slap on the wrist."

She stared at him. "But why go into it if you think you might lose?"

"Both Linda and I think it's worth it, because of the other kids still out on the streets." He fixed his gaze on her face, dreading her reaction to what he had to say next. "I intend to use every kind of cheap trick I can think of to generate publicity during this trial, hoping to demonstrate how badly we need to do something for those runaways."

Merle stared at him silently, absorbing what he had said, running it through her mind. When the implications became clear, she got up and began to pace around the office with quick, graceful movements, her skirt swishing around her knees with each step.

Affected in a way that wasn't particularly productive at this point, Shane clasped his hands around his knee again and turned his gaze toward the window. But he could still hear the whisper of her clothes moving against her body. Everything would be so much simpler if her very presence on this earth didn't have such a powerful effect on him, he thought.

It took him by surprise when she stopped in front of him and curled her fingers around his wrists. "We're like oil and water, aren't we? We just don't mix," she said sadly.

He touched her cheeks with his fingertips, her hands still on his wrists. "Merry, I love you. Do you believe that?"

She stared at him, studying his face. "Yes . . . yes, I think I do." She hesitated for a moment, then said in a low voice, "I think I must love you too, Shane." Tears welled up and rolled down her cheeks. "But it's so useless."

"Maybe." Bending his head, he kissed first one tear away and then the other. "But we're awfully good together. I guess we proved that yesterday, didn't we?"

"We're good that way, I'll agree." There was no humor in her slight smile, not when her large brown eyes were filled with sadness. "That's the only time we don't fight—when we're in bed."

"It's something though, isn't it? It must mean there's a chance for us, don't you think?"

Lowering her eyes, she stared at his chest and detoured around the question. "I think what you told me a few minutes ago is that you intend to encourage a media feeding frenzy all the way through the trial. Is that right?"

Shane wished to hell he could deny it. He lifted his shoulders in a shrug and held them up for a few seconds.

"Miss Merry won't survive any more publicity—if she's weathered this first dose." Her expression was almost desperate as she looked up into his eyes. "Miss Merry and my girls are my life, Shane. I can't throw them away."

It sounded too much like the beginning of the end, and he couldn't bear the thought of losing her again. He clasped his fingers around the nape of her neck as if he could hold her. "I know, I understand, but if we wait for a little while, say until after you come back from your tour, it should be safe for us to see each other. We'd have to be careful no one catches us, that's all."

Merle pulled back in frustration. "Oh, I hate this! I refuse to sneak around and have a tawdry affair with you."

His sense of helplessness set the demons inside him off again. "Tawdry affair! *I* saw what we shared yesterday as something a little more transcendent than a tawdry affair."

Narrowing her eyes, she peered into his self-righteous face for a second, then lifted the sides of his jacket to expose his red T-shirt. "Well, Mr. High-and-Mighty *Legal Stud*, the way *I* see it—if we can't have an open, aboveboard relationship, there's no hope." Wrinkling her patrician nose, she repeated, "Legal stud?! I'll bet some woman gave you that shirt."

He sheepishly pulled his jacket together. "Never mind my shirt, I'm not giving you up, Merry."

Her expression was serious again. "Remember what we talked about in Riley's Place? About my being afraid of being hurt and you saying you couldn't love and didn't want to give a woman a half a loaf? There are so many things stacked against us."

Agonizingly, he touched her cheek, then her lips with a fingertip. "I wouldn't ever want to hurt you, darlin'. But there's got to be a way for us to make a life together."

"I wish, I wish." She kissed his fingertip, then slowly shook her head.

Putting his arms around her waist, he pulled her closer. "I'll back out of Linda's case. Barney can take over. You're more important to me than anything else."

She stiffened in his arms. "If you do, I'll definitely call it quits, Shane Halloran! What you're doing is too important to throw away!"

He set his mouth to argue, then decided that would be the worst possible tactic. "Okay, okay, I've got another plan—it's not perfect, but it's something. Maybe we can put everything on hold until the trial is over. Then we'll be free to talk out our problems and see what we can build together. What do you think?"

Merle hesitated long enough to put him through torture. Finally she slipped her fingers under the leather collar of his jacket and said, "That's a possibility. When will the trial be over?"

He let out the breath he'd been holding. "I wish I could predict. It could be over by the time you come back from your tour. Or it could run on for months."

"So long?"

"I'm afraid so."

She sighed deeply and brushed his lips with a kiss. "Well, at least we'll be able to see each other at Ellen's wedding."

Then she pulled free, swung around, and left the office before Shane could think of a way to stop her. He remained motionless on the edge of his desk for several minutes, picturing the four months until the end of July and the wedding stretching out before him like a wasteland.

His only consolation was that at least she hadn't closed the door on him. There was hope.

Six

Dear Miss Merry,
I'm fifteen and I don't have anyone to talk to. I can't tell my mom, she'd have a cow. I know you always tell us to just say no, but early in May me and my boyfriend did it anyway. Can a girl get pregnant if it just happens once? How can I tell if I am? Please hurry and answer because I'm real scared.

Cindy Jones

My dear Cindy,
Love, I'll answer your letter privately and immediately. I know I always tell you to say no, but I also understand how easy it is to surrender to temptation. Yes, unfortunately a girl can get pregnant after doing it just once. You might suspect you're pregnant if you miss your menstrual period, or feel nauseous in the morning. Your breasts will . . .

Cindy's letter had taken top priority as soon as Merle read it that morning. It was already the fourth week of July, so if the girl was pregnant, she'd be more than two months along. Merle filled two pages with comfort, support, and advice, including the address for a counseling center in her city and a strong suggestion that she speak to her mother. After printing the letter out, she stuffed it in an envelope and set it aside to send by overnight mail.

"What are you doing here so early?" Louise asked, walking into the office carrying a bakery sack and take-out coffee.

Merle reached for the ceiling, stretching her tired body. She was dressed in blue pants and a flowered blouse, quite a difference in professional attire for her. "I couldn't sleep, so I thought I might as well come in early and catch up on some things rather than lie awake thinking about . . . this and that."

Louise sat down at her desk and took an almond Danish out of the bakery sack, put it on a napkin, and held it out to Merle. "Here, these are decadently fattening and good for anything that ails you."

Merle's stomach did a flip-flop over the sharp, bittersweet aroma of almonds. Swallowing convulsively, she jumped up and retreated out of range of the smell. "No, I couldn't."

"Good Lord, I've never actually seen anyone turn green before." Louise withdrew her hand and took a bite of the pastry herself, frowning at Merle. "I've been nagging you about looking terrible for weeks now. What's wrong?"

"Oh, it's nothing. I'm still fighting the aftereffects of that funny flu I picked up on my speaking tour, that's all. It's a Martian variety, I think, because it takes the constitution of a robot to survive it." Merle pressed her fingers against her unreliable stomach. "There can't be anything seriously wrong with me, because Ellen's wedding is this coming Saturday, and I *am* going, no matter what."

Louise popped the last bite of Danish into her mouth and threw her balled napkin into the wastebasket. "Why don't you go to the doctor and get yourself checked out?"

Merle stared through the window. A good steady summer sun was shining, glittering on the choppy waves of the ocean. No fog. The air was so clear, she could have seen the Farallon Islands if she hadn't been so preoccupied. She glanced back at Louise. "If it isn't the flu, then it's probably just stress. Heaven knows I've had plenty of that in the last few months."

"What stress is bothering you now? Not the picture in the paper, surely."

"No, the media forgot all about the mystery woman early in April, when that Marin County mud slide took five houses with it."

Louise gave a laugh. "Such a fortuitous disaster—do you have an in up above?"

"Not likely, the way things are going." Merle rocked back in her chair, nervously rubbing the dimple in her chin. "No, I'm not particularly worried about the media. Shane and his case are provocative enough to keep them satisfied."

Loneliness joined the queasiness at the pit of her stomach when she thought about Shane, Mr. Stress himself. His trial had been dragging on for four months. Hollbrook and his upper-echelon lawyers had been throwing up roadblocks, delays, and postponements at every opportunity, trying to wear him down.

He called often on the phone, but she'd seen him only once, just within the last week. And even then they'd kept it casual and polite.

"Last Friday Rob's family hosted the rehearsal dinner," Merle said, clasping her hands in her lap. "Ellen wanted me to come, and Shane was there, of course, because she asked him to give her away. Quite a few other Hallorans were there, too, so it turned out to be wild and rambunctious. I swear they all laugh and talk at the tops of their voices—simultaneously. Ellen fell right into it—must be genetic. Actually, everyone had a ball but me. Well, I had fun for a while, until I passed out."

"You *what?*" Louise leaned forward, frowning. "Good Lord! You weren't drunk, were you?"

"*No!* You know I don't drink. I couldn't stand the smell of seafood, and then the men lit up cigars and the air got close, so I just conked out, that's all. But Shane overreacted and bundled me down to the emergency room, with half the party trailing along. It was mortifying."

Merle rubbed her forehead with her fingertips. "They did an EKG and assured everyone I hadn't had a heart attack, then sent me home with orders to call my doctor the next morning. I did, and Dr. Shapiro ordered a whole battery of tests. Now I'm waiting for the results to come back."

Louise's face showed her concern. "Did he say what he thought it might be?"

Merle bit her lip and stared at her hands, clasped so tightly the knuckles were white. "He can't be sure until the test results come back, but—" She looked up, her eyes panicked. "Oh, Louise, he thinks I might have a tumor. Even worse than that, he thinks I might be going into an early menopause. But I'm not even forty! I'm not ready to be old yet!" She burst into tears. "I feel as if I'm walking on a tightrope, waiting to hear."

On Saturday Merle knew the test results, and now she felt as if she were walking a tightrope over the Grand Canyon in a stiff wind. Her anxiety had transformed into disbelief, spiced with a little horror. If she let her guard down for even a moment, hope and anticipation tended to sneak in. And either of those were unrealistic to the point of being ridiculous. She only knew one thing for certain; for this very special day she had to put her own dilemma aside and concentrate on her daughter's happiness.

She arrived at the church two hours before the service was scheduled and found Ellen on the verge of tears, pacing in the bride's room in a bouffant slip and a lace bra. Her attendants were hovering ineffectively around her, a matron of honor in deep rose and three bridesmaids in baby-pink dresses with tulip skirts.

Merle sent them out and asked Ellen, "What's wrong, darling?"

Ellen started to cry. "I don't know if I'm really, really doing the right thing in marrying Rob."

Feeling a great surge of maternal love, Merle gathered her daughter into her arms. "You were sure as you've always been at the rehearsal dinner. Has something happened since then? Has Rob done something to hurt you?"

"Nothing—of course not. Down deep I know I'm sure." A self-mocking, twisted smile came and went on Ellen's face. "I thought I, of all people, would be immune to the last-minute jitters. I just needed my mummy, I guess. You still look pale, what did the doctor say?" she asked anxiously.

Merle's smile froze. Her heart jumped. It wasn't the time or the place for revelations, so she cleared her throat and said evasively, "Basically he said I'm healthy enough to see you through a dozen weddings."

"A dozen! I'm not sure I'll make it through this one." Ellen drew in a deep breath. "One step at a time, right? This is the first step." She pinned a pink rosebud corsage to Merle's shoulder, then stood back and smiled. "You look beautiful."

"Why, thank you, love." Merle brushed at the floaty material of her dress, a pale lavender with a pattern of rose-colored flowers. "But why don't we get you dressed now and find out just how beautiful a woman really can be." She called the others back in and let the bridal attendant take over to orchestrate the final countdown.

A few minutes before four P.M. Merle left the dressing room. A gray-tuxedoed usher escorted her down the aisle of the wedding chapel, with its domed ceiling and masses of white vine orchids in front of an elaborate altar. The western sun blazed through the stained glass windows in jewellike colors. Love songs vibrated from a muted pipe organ. Most of the pews were already filled with whispering guests in festive clothes.

She sat down in the front pew on the left. Shane's sister, brothers, and their spouses were sitting in the pew behind her, with numerous aunts, uncles, and cousins behind them. On Merle's left in the front pew were his parents. They smiled at Merle, then Maggie Halloran leaned close and whispered, "Did you find out what caused your spell?"

Merle felt heat pinken her face. Until now it hadn't occurred to her how bizarre her current situation might appear to other people. "It was nothing . . . serious."

The old woman smiled. "We've been wanting to tell you, my Pat and me, how warmly we feel toward you. We never thought we'd have a grandchild from our Shane, and here you've given us Ellen."

Merle managed a nod and a twisted smile, then turned away to watch the pastor and Rob, in a white tuxedo, appear at the altar, followed by his groomsmen. The organ picked up volume in a processional, and the bridesmaids floated like rose petals down the aisle.

A shiver ran down Merle's spine and goose bumps broke out on her arms when the organist segued into the wedding march. A lump lodged in her throat as her daughter began walking in measured cadence down the aisle, face veiled, train spread out behind, her hand on Shane's arm. He looked so handsome in his gray tuxedo that Merle could hardly bear to look at him. At the foot of the altar he solemnly agreed to "give this woman" and handed Ellen over to Rob.

Then he sat down beside Merle in the front pew, his eyes sparkling. "How'd I do?" he whispered.

"It was as if you were born to it." *Born to it.* She frowned slightly, wondering what the fates had been thinking to gift this man with such a unique talent for confusing her life.

A contralto began singing "Oh Promise Me." Shane gazed at Merle. "You look too young and glamorous to be the mother of a bride." His smile died. "But you still look pale. Did the doctor get the test results back?"

The woman's singing swelled, covering the rustle when Merle fumbled with her clutch purse and dropped it on the floor. Shane bent over and retrieved it, his expression worried when she didn't answer. "Merry, what's wrong with you?" he whispered harshly.

She leaned over, her lips close to his ear. "Nothing! I'm healthy as a horse, I swear. Now, will you be quiet? I want to listen to the ceremony."

The pastor began delivering a sermon. "Ellen, Rob, marriage should not be entered into lightly. . . ."

Maggie Halloran began to snuffle. A couple of other Halloran women joined in. Merle felt her throat closing up and drew in a long, quivery breath, then bit her lip for control.

Shane nudged her with an elbow, grinning as he held out a large white handkerchief. "Bet you didn't come prepared for an Irish wedding."

"Shhh!" She bit back a laugh and dabbed her eyes with the handkerchief.

"There is no problem that cannot be overcome," the pastor intoned, "if both partners are willing to search for a solution, honestly and openly, with unselfish love."

Merle glanced sidelong at Shane, wondering how they could possibly solve their problems when things were escalating from impossible to horrendous. He felt her gaze on him and turned to meet her eyes, his expression solemn, his hand closing on hers as the pastor began speaking the age-old traditional vows that Ellen had chosen to use.

". . . do you take this man to be your lawful husband . . ."

Fantasies and dreams could be built upon those words. Merle's spirits soared as she threaded her fingers through Shane's.

". . . promise to love, honor, and cherish . . ."

Her lips curved in a tremulous smile; his lips quivered in an answering one.

". . . for richer or for poorer, through sickness and health . . . ?"

For that moment the two of them, Merle and Shane, were alone in the church, in the world. For that moment all her confusion and anxiety faded away. She accepted it now, that it was really true love for him she felt radiating up from her soul to glow in her eyes.

"I do."

Her heart ached for what might have been between them. Tears trickled unnoticed down her cheeks.

". . . do you take this woman . . ."

Shane moved his lips silently with the words.

". . . to love, honor, and cherish . . ."

His expression was serious and tender.

"Until death do you part?"

"I do."

"I now pronounce you husband and wife. You may kiss the bride."

He brushed his lips against Merle's. For a second they gazed into each other's eyes, bound together by their star-crossed love and agonized yearning.

Then they turned to watch Rob lift their daughter's veil and give her a rousing, full-bodied buss while the guests applauded vigorously. The organist struck up the recessional. Beaming, hand in hand, the young couple strode away from the altar, followed by their attendants.

Merle pulled her hand away from Shane's, wipe
her cheeks with his handkerchief, and handed i
back. They got up and followed the wedding party t
the vestibule. Laughing and crying, she hugged he
daughter. "And now you're Mrs. Taylor. Oh, m
sweet, I'm so happy for you."

Turning Ellen over to Shane, Merle threw her arm
around Rob. "You take good care of my baby, hear?

He laughed happily. "Don't worry, I love her mor
than life itself."

Ellen took Merle's hand. "It'd be fun to have yo
stand in the receiving line with me. But I'll under
stand if you'd rather not."

Caught up in the excitement and love of the mo
ment, Merle didn't hesitate a second. "There's n
place I'd rather be than right beside you, love."

Shane gave her a grin and a squeeze. "Welcome t
the real world, darlin'. Have you finally discovere
some things are more important than that reputa
tion of yours?"

She made a face at him. "My reputation has been i
tatters since the first minute I laid eyes on you. An
you don't even know the half of it yet."

The guests made their way slowly down the line i
a pandemonium of hasty introductions, hand shak
ing, cheek kissing, laughter, and shrieks from both
Ellen's and Rob's friends and relatives. When the en
was in sight, Merle breathed a sigh of relief that n
one had openly questioned her presence in the line

Then she gave a horrified gasp when she saw th
woman tagging along at the very end of the crowd–
Valerie Valerto, a society editor for the *Chronicle*
ultrachic in a royal blue dress and hat. After congrat
ulating Rob and Ellen, Valerie took Merle's hand an
didn't let go, beaming a brilliant smile. "Why Merle
darling, what an incredible surprise to see you in
place like this! This lovely young bride must b
your . . . what? Dear friend? Your niece?"

The people who had been milling around fell silent

watching and listening. Obviously they'd all wondered.

The time for running and hiding was past. Merle took Ellen's hand. "Val, I'm very proud to introduce my daughter, Mrs. Ellen Taylor." There, it was over. She smiled, feeling a sense of relief and freedom.

"Why, *darling!* I didn't know you had children. How wonderful, how exciting." Valerie smiled at Ellen. "Merle and I have known each other, lo these many years—we were cubs together. People in publishing are like one big family, you know. But I do believe she's been holding out on us."

Valerie's gaze flickered over Shane's silvered black hair, sparkling blue eyes, and full-power grin, then down over his body to his polished gray shoes. Her laughter was bell-like. "Merle darling, who *is* this scrumptious man standing beside you?"

Merle's shoulders drooped. "You know perfectly well who this scrumptious man is, Val."

"Oh, of course, I've been following your case with bated breath, Mr. Halloran."

The photographer began herding the wedding party away for pictures then, giving Merle a reprieve. She grabbed Valerie's arm and steered her into a private corner. "Val, what *are* you doing here?"

"Now, now, don't be upset. You've been a reporter yourself, so you know one has to track down a story wherever one can. I recognized you the instant I saw that interesting photo last March, so I nosed around until everything fell together. How'd you come up with a daughter, of all things?"

Merle sighed. "I had Ellen when I was a teen and gave her up for adoption. We found each other again last spring."

"How fascinating! It's fairly obvious who her father is. I've never seen two such identical smiles. Why don't we set up a date for an interview, and you can tell all."

Merle pictured her precious privacy and her career

disintegrating. "Val, please don't write this story. Surely you can see the impact it'll have on Miss Merry."

"Darling, these are the nineties, not Victorian times. Everyone who is anyone does single parenting nowadays. A story about your experience might even enhance your career. If I don't do the story, someone else is bound to. I'm a friend, at least I'll be accurate and sympathetic."

Merle couldn't stave off defeat. "All right, call my office next week, and I'll see what we can set up."

Shane popped up then. "Come on, Merry, they're waiting for you."

Val gave him a flirty smile. "Aren't you just a living doll!" Then she clicked briskly out of the church on three-inch heels.

Merle made it through the rest of the evening in a daze. She survived the sit-down dinner by pushing her food around her plate with her fork. She held her breath as she touched her lip to the champagne for the toasts. She laughed when Ellen cut the cake and jammed a bite in Rob's mouth, winced when he reciprocated, applauded when the bouquet and garter were tossed, threw rice when Ellen ran with Rob to their beribboned and tin-canned car.

Then, as if by magic, the wedding guests left and there was blessed quiet as she stood beside Shane outside the banquet room, under the stars. "Well, that's over," he said, slipping off his cravat and opening the top button of his shirt. "It was a beautiful wedding, wasn't it?"

"Oh, yes," she said softly. "Beautiful and touching."

Taking her hand, he drew her into the shadows and put his arms around her. His eyes glowed as he looked at her. "This wedding seemed particularly meaningful, didn't you think?"

She put her arms around his neck, smiling teasingly. "Because it was our daughter?"

He grinned. "You know what I mean, I can see it in your face. It should have been us up there."

"Oh, I wish . . ."

He clasped his hands behind her waist, his grin fading. "We've already shared the vows, why don't we drive up to Tahoe tonight and make it legal?"

She peered into his face, numbed by the possibility. "You're serious, aren't you?" she said uncertainly.

"I've never been more serious in my life." He lifted the wispy, free-hanging lavender panel of her dress. "You look like a bride in this dress. Let's do it."

The impulse to say yes was strong, she even opened her mouth to agree, then bit off the words. "Marriage vows are supposed to be forever, Shane. They aren't something to take lightly."

He cupped her cheek with one big hand. "Believe me, I don't. Whatever it is that's pulling us together is so strong, I don't understand it."

She searched his face for a moment, agonizing, then turned her head and kissed his palm. "My darling, I don't understand it either. But I do know I don't want to jump into something and have it end in failure. We've got too many problems to resolve before we can think about marriage."

Shane sighed in reluctant acceptance. "I suppose you're right, but it was a interesting idea."

She nodded, smiling tremulously. "Oh, yes."

"Someday we'll make it, darlin'. Just you wait and see." He pulled her close and lowered his head, claiming her lips.

For the first time Merle didn't respond full-force to his kiss. She was too tired, her stomach too queasy. Dropping her head on his shoulder, she sighed from the bottom of her lungs.

"What was that sigh all about?" Shane put his fingers under her chin and lifted her face toward the light. "Merry, you look as if you've been wrung through a wringer. I don't believe you're as okay as you've been insisting."

She pulled out of his arms. It was on the tip of her tongue to tell him about the test results, but it wouldn't be fair to flip something like that at him as an afterthought to a full day. Besides, she didn't know what she thought about it herself. "It's nothing, I'm just exhausted. I need to go home and fall in bed."

His brows came down. "I don't believe you, there's something else."

"Just drop it, Shane—okay? Trust me, I *am* all right." Merle walked across the lighted parking lot.

He walked beside her, kicking at scatterings of rice, obviously not convinced. When she reached her car, he watched her fumble in her clutch purse for her keys. "What happens now that the Valerto woman knows your secret? What's she going to do with it?"

The question came at her so unexpectedly, she dropped her keychain. "Oh, I wish you hadn't reminded me of that. I'd forgotten about Val in all the excitement. I suppose she'll write an article, slanted toward what it's like to rediscover a child after so many years."

Shane picked up the keys and unlocked the car, helped Merle behind the wheel, tucked her skirt in, then rested an arm on the top of the door. "Since everything is coming into the open, can we start seeing each other again?"

Merle took a deep breath and glanced sidelong at him. "I have a feeling you'll be seeing a lot more of me than you bargained for. Why don't you drop by my house for lunch tomorrow? There's something I have to tell you."

even

Dear Miss Merry,

I just found out my mother and dad got pregnant with me and had to get married. I don't think they even loved each other, because all they ever do is fight. They blame each other for me. Do you think they'd be happier if I ran away?

Desolate

Dear Desolate,

No, darling, your parents wouldn't be happier if you ran away. Their fighting is about their own inner unhappiness, not about you. They'll only be happier if they learn to communicate openly with each other. It might help all of you if you tell them how you feel. Write to me again, my sweet. I care.

Miss Merry

The next afternoon Merle was waiting at the win-ow in the living room of her house, wearing a pair of hite pedal pushers and a fuchsia overblouse. The cent of rose-petal potpourri mingled with the fresh

air wafting in through an open window. Despite th
comfort and coziness of the room, her emotions wer
hitting so many peaks and valleys, they would hav
looked like the Alps on a graph.

She still hadn't thought of a way to tell Shane.
cold sweat broke out on her body when she saw hi
turn off the access road on his motorcycle and begi
weaving and swaying up her steep driveway. Taking
deep breath, she left the window and stood in th
open doorway to watch him dismount and take o
his helmet.

"Hullo, darlin'," he said, his grin unsuspecting a
he stepped into the entry and reached out to curv
his fingers under her upper arms, pulling her close

It was tempting to melt into the comfort of hi
embrace, but she steeled herself to ward him off. "N
hugs—if we get too friendly, I won't be able to thin
straight, and we've got something awfully importa
to discuss."

He dropped his arms and pushed his hands int
his jean pockets, his grin fading. "Things can't b
quite as ominous as you're making them sound,
hope."

"As far as I can tell, life in general is ominous
Come in and let's get this over with."

She led him into her living room, then perched o
the edge of the sofa to watch nervously as he hun
his black leather jacket on the wing of an armchai
His T-shirt was blue, green, and white and bore th
logo Save the Earth. Finally he sat down on the othe
end of the sofa, turned sideways with a knee draw
up. "Okay, spew it out. What's chewing on you?"

She swallowed dryly. "I'm pregnant."

"Say *what?!*" He stared blankly at her for a fe
seconds. Then he had the audacity to laugh. "You'r
kidding."

"Shane Halloran, don't you dare laugh at me!" Sh
threw a ruffled pillow at him.

He caught it. "You're *not* kidding!"

She shook her head, her wavy hair swaying around her neck.

Tossing the pillow aside, he ran his hands through his hair, then over the back of his neck. "I don't know what to say. Knock me down with a feather."

"It's more like being hit on the head with a hammer."

"But I thought you couldn't get pregnant."

"I can't. I mean I couldn't! But no one ever pinpointed the reason for my not conceiving, so my doctor is guessing the problem must have been psychological. All I had to do was get with you again, and . . ." She raised her hands, palms up. "I think we must be hexed or something, Shane."

He grimaced apologetically. "Sorry I laughed when you first told me, it didn't sink in." Then he glanced at her, chin lifted, backtracking in his head. "You must have known this for a while. Why didn't you tell me as soon as you suspected?"

"I haven't been hiding anything from you! I only just found out when the tests came back, day before the wedding. I didn't say anything yesterday because I didn't want to ruin Ellen's special day. And because I hadn't accepted the idea myself and didn't know how to talk about it." She made a face. "I still don't, but . . ."

"Yeah, it's a blockbuster, all right." Straightening himself on the sofa, Shane crossed one ankle over the other knee and picked at the hem of his jean leg, brows lowered. Then a smile began on his lips, budding and blossoming into a full-fledged grin. He glanced up. "You know, this is really kind of wonderful."

"Wonderful?" Yearning stirred in her breast. If only, if only . . . but how? "There are a dozen arguments against its being wonderful," she said sadly, and jumped up to walk across the room and stare out window, chilled despite the summery sunshine beaming down outside.

Shane got up and stood beside her, leaning one broad shoulder against the window frame. "But I thought you always wanted to get pregnant and be a mother."

Frustration, mixed feelings, and the paradoxical unfairness of the situation put an edge in her voice. "Sure, I wanted to be—more than anything! But that was when I was in my twenties and early thirties. If this had happened ten years ago, or even five, I would have been delirious with joy. But everything's different now. I'm not married, on top of the list. I don't even have a family around to help out—not that they were much help when . . ."

She gave a humorless laugh. "I'm not sure I'd be much of a blessing to a baby. What kind of mother would I make? I've been Miss Merry so long, I've turned into a universal old-maid aunt."

Anxiety flushed her pale cheeks. "And what about Miss Merry? What's going to happen to her if people find out I'm pregnant? Ye gods, look how ecstatic Valerie Valerto was over nosing out Ellen! Just think what'd happen if she saw me out to here." She circled her arms far out in front of her belly. "I can see the headline already. Miss Merry pregnant again—by the same man! And don't think for one minute my bosses at *Youngest Sister* won't see it too. Not to mention the parents of my young fans."

Shane listened patiently to her tirade, brows down, pinching his lower lip, and when she paused for breath, he conceded, "Granted, there may be a complication or two."

She barely heard him as a different, far more troublesome problem drained the color out of her face. "But it's not my job that worries me so much as the fact that I'm almost forty," she said, wrapping her arms around her body. "My biological clock is awfully close to running out. A dozen things could go wrong, each one more scary than the next."

Shane took her shoulders and turned her toward

im so he could search her face. "Is pregnancy
langerous for you, sweetheart? I don't think I could
tand it if anything happened to you."

She unwrapped her arms and waved his concern
ff. "No, no, I'm fine. I swear I had every test known to
nedicine done in the last week, and the results are
roof that I'm in bounding good health."

He peered at her. "You don't look very healthy to
ne. Your eyes look like burnt-match smudges in your
ace."

She bent her head and shook her light gold hair
orward to hide her pallor. "I look this way because
've felt sick for four months, and I haven't slept a full
ight since I first saw the doctor."

"Merry, why didn't you *tell* me you weren't feeling
ood when we talked on the phone all these
nonths?" he demanded, anxiety making him sound
s irritable as she did. "I didn't realize anything was
oing on until you passed out at the rehearsal din-
er."

She glanced at him, her chin quivering. "How
ould you expect me to tell you about the gross
hysical things that were happening to me? We
ardly know each other, other than being lovers."

Shane put his fingers under her chin and forced
er to look at him. "Listen, I'm going to see to it that
ou have the best doctors and medical care available.
won't let anything happen to you."

"I've got the best doctor already! I've been going to
im forever, and I wouldn't think of having anyone
lse." She pulled away from him, struggling for con-
rol. "It isn't my health I'm worried about. I've been
ying awake trying to decide what I should do about
he pregnancy."

"Do about it! What can you do about it, but have—"
hane broke off when he remembered there were
nore choices than the obvious one. He took a deep
reath and blew it out through his lips. "This is more

than a pregnancy, Merry. This is our baby. Just exactly what options *are* you thinking about?"

Baby. Merle had forbidden herself to think about that part of it. She couldn't, not when she felt so strongly it was wrong to bring a precious little innocent into anything but a complete family life. Regret and longing caused her to flare out bitterly at Shane. "The options are exactly the same as when I was pregnant with Ellen."

Suddenly the emotional pain and grief she'd buried so long ago came surging up to join the current worry, tipping the scale too far. She folded her arms over her midriff and hugged herself, feeling like a frightened, deserted sixteen-year-old again. "Shane, it's happening all over again! I . . . don't think I can stand to go . . . through this again! It was too hard when I had to—" She burst into tears, her body wracked by great convulsive sobs.

"Aw, Merry . . . aw, honey." Shane gathered her into his arms, pressing her close, patting and stroking her back while she saturated the word "Earth" on his T-shirt with her tears. "Merry, don't . . . don't . . . shhh. Don't cry like this, it can't be good for you. . . . Shhh."

Gradually the storm passed, and she leaned against him, trembling as the last spasms of sobbing subsided into gasps and hiccuping. She pressed her face against the beating of his strong, steady heart. "I'm so confused and scared. My whole life is going into a flip-flop, and I don't know what to think or what to do."

"Merry, you're not alone this time," he said, his lips moving against her forehead, his hand gently smoothing her hair. "We got into this together, darlin', and we'll see it through together. Everything is going to be all right, I promise."

"I want to believe you, but—" She gave a great shuddering sigh.

"No buts, Darlin'. One way or another, we're going

to get through this and still be standing on top o' the world, just you wait and see." His stroking hands on her back found and counted her ribs. "Merry, you feel like a frail little bird in my arms. I don't think I saw you eat a bite of food at the reception last night. When *is* the last time you ate a solid meal?"

"I don't know, I can't hold anything down. I've been nauseated for . . . oh, I don't know how long. It seems like forever." Tears started flowing again. "I must look like a hag."

Shane slipped his fingers under her chin and lifted her face. "You've never looked more beautiful to me."

"You always say that. How can I believe a word you say?"

"Ask me, does it matter how you look? I don't care." He kissed the tears off her lashes. "Tell you what, you go wash your face and pretty yourself up. I'll find the kitchen and fix you something to eat."

"Don't look at me, my eyes are still puffy," Merle said when she walked into the kitchen fifteen minutes later, her face made up and her hair combed. "Do I look awful?"

"Worse than something the tide washed up," Shane said cheerfully, then ducked and laughed when she snapped her finger at his nose. "Make up your mind, darlin'. A minute ago you were complaining that I always say you're beautiful."

She gave her first genuine laugh in what seemed like months. "If you'd learn to moderate, love, maybe we wouldn't always be in trouble."

"I'm moderating already. See, I'm not rising to the bait with a comeback, I'm not starting a fight, now am I?"

She laughed again. "Not as long as I keep *my* mouth shut."

He grinned, then escorted her into the sunroom off

the kitchen and pulled a chair out from the table. "Sit down and make yourself at home."

Merle obediently sat on the edge of the chair, but her stomach bucked at the thought of food. "Don't feel hurt if I can't eat anything."

"Trust me," he said, laying a place mat, silverware, and napkin in front of her. "In my family one or another of the women are always pregnant, and even when they aren't, that's all they talk about. I've picked up a trick or two along the way."

Taking one slice of toast out of the toaster, he quartered it and spread jam on it, put it on a plate, and set it in front of her. "No tea, no coffee, no liquid of any kind until you get this down. After that we play it by ear."

Sitting across from her, he leaned a chin on his fist and looked out the window. "Looks as if your house is still sitting here on top of the hill, so our plastic raincoat job must have worked. What you really ought to do is put in a series of terraces with piers to hold the earth in place before winter comes again." While he carried on his one-sided conversation, Merle took a tentative nibble of toast. It went down all right, so she took a few more.

"That's one advantage of a houseboat, it stays put," he rambled on. "Unless, of course, you spring a leak; that could lead to some nasty surprises. And earthquakes make for an interesting shake, rattle, and slosh. Worse than a local earthquake would be one in Alaska or somewhere that might start a tsunami. If that happened, I might end up in your backyard. Did you know, last time a tsunami was predicted people actually went down to the beach to watch for the tidal wave? Talk about stupid."

Merle smiled over his patter, forgetting the jumbled worries she'd been carrying alone for so long. She finished the toast and felt a stir of appetite. "Maybe I could manage another slice. If you're still cooking."

"Your wish is my command." Shane got up and

walked into the kitchen, with its copper kettles hanging overhead and the greenhouse window above the sink filled with vines and African violets. "Would it be safe for me to say this is a pretty fancy house you have here?" he asked, still making light conversation. "Miss Merry must do all right."

"She does okay, but not that great. It's just that this house is all I have to spend my money on." She frowned thoughtfully, her stomach tensing. "At least up until this year she's done okay, but I don't know what's going to happen to Miss Merry now, much less my house, when . . . if . . ."

"Darlin', let's don't be countin' our troubles before they sprout. You're not alone, remember?"

Shane rambled on about a variety of subjects while Merle ate three more slices of toast and drank a glass of apple juice. "Better quit while you're ahead," he finally said. He cleared her place and sat down again, leaning his elbows on the table. "There. Now maybe we can get to the bottom of this problem of ours. First off, when's the baby due?"

Her chin jerked up as if he'd hit her with the word—baby. The notion of a baby seemed so unreal, she couldn't grasp it in her mind. "When? I don't know. But there's only one time I could have gotten pregnant—the end of March, when we—" A sudden thought struck her. She leaned forward and peered at him. "Shane, please believe me when I say you're the only one who could have . . ." She flipped her hand.

He reached across the table to touch her face. "Merry, I know you at least that well. This happened only because we're special together."

She gave a relieved, slightly wry smile. "I'm not sure if we're special or disastrous."

"There's a possibility it's a toss-up," he conceded. "But, anyway, if it's from the end of March—" he counted down nine fingers, "it'll be the end of December. Our baby is going to be a little Capricorn. How about that?"

"A Capricorn?" She frowned, wishing he wouldn't give the baby a personality. It made everything so much more difficult. The decisions she had to make would be easier if she could simply think of it as a pregnancy.

He turned sideways, legs stretched out, one elbow on the back of the chair and one on the table. "Okay, let's talk about those options," he said, looking at her a little defiantly. "What are they, outside of the obvious?"

Merle turned her head and looked out the window. "Well . . . I'm over four months along, so my doctor says it's urgent that I decide as soon as possible whether I want to go through with . . . this."

Shane pulled in his legs and straightened himself around, clasping his hands on the table. "Surely you aren't seriously thinking about terminating the pregnancy?"

"I don't know!" she cried out. Even though the thought made her feel sick, a termination was something she had to at least consider at her age. "I don't know what the right thing is."

Shane frowned at his hands for a few moments, then glanced up. "You wouldn't terminate just for convenience' sake, would you?"

All her mixed feelings caused her to flare out at him in irrational anger. "*Convenience?!* This is a terrible decision to make—how dare you think I might do it lightly and selfishly!" She glared at him with smoldering dark eyes. "For your information, I can't think of anything sadder than bringing an unwanted child into the world."

"This child isn't unwanted," he said, thrusting his head forward. "I had fifty-fifty responsibility in setting this thing off, so I have some rights here, too, you know. If you don't want the baby, I do."

"I never said I didn't *want* it!" she exclaimed

furiously. She couldn't resist the truth any longer; she wanted the baby more than anything else in the world. "But I'd be a fool to attempt single parenting without examining the future. I have to look at every option and try to think of what might be best for the baby—as well as myself. For Pete's sake, Shane—think about it!" she cried desperately, as much to remind herself as him. "I'll be sixty years old before the baby's grown up!"

He lifted his chin. "Well, I for one intend to be young yet at sixty, and I don't feel any particular qualms about being a single parent. So why don't you have the baby and give it to me?"

Merle glared at him and yanked her fuchsia over-blouse down, resting a possessive hand over her rounded belly. "Let me see if I understand this. You're suggesting I go through pregnancy and delivery as some kind of a . . . a . . . surrogate mother for you? I'll bet you'd be singing a different tune if it were *you* getting fatter and more miserable. I'd like to hear *you* try to explain your little slip to your clients, the judges, and juries."

His face reddened at her challenge. "If there's one thing I'm sure of, it's that my reputation would be the last thing I'd worry about if I were pregnant."

She poked the table with a stiff forefinger. "Let me tell you this, Mr. Equal Rights Halloran. Say I did go through with this pregnancy." She hesitated, the reality dawning on her. Not only did she want the baby, but it was real. Hers. Her eyes narrowed in a fierce expression. "H–e–double toothpicks would have to freeze over before I'd hand *my* baby over to you."

He leaned forward and scowled at her. "Dammit, Merry, you cheated me out of my first baby, and I refuse to give this one up too."

"*You* were cheated?!" She jumped to her feet, trembling with anger, and leaned forward on her knuckles. "You've got some gall, Shane Halloran, after you've done this to me not once but *twice*!"

He jumped up too, his chair toppling behind him. "What do you mean, *I* did it to you? It takes two, you know."

A few moments of silence fell.

He took a deep breath and unhunched his shoulders. "Why in hell am I bellowing at you at a time like this?"

Merle stared at him, breathing through her mouth as her anger slowly evaporated. "Probably because I goaded you into it, I suppose." She shook her head apologetically, sadly. "Oh, Shane, why can't we ever discuss anything, *anything*, without our tempers exploding?"

"The only excuse I can come up with is that it must have been my demons talking again," he said, running both hands through his hair. "I'm beginning to think I need an exorcist."

Coming around the table, he took Merle in his arms and kissed her on the forehead. "I shouldn't have tried to bulldoze you. I always thought no one could believe more strongly than I do in the rights of the individual. You, in this case." He gave her a wry smile. "It would seem I just found out that equal rights are a hell of a lot easier to support when they don't affect me personally. Will you accept my apology?"

"Only if you'll accept mine." She put her arms around his waist and pressed her face into his chest. "I don't know why I tried to shut you out—that's the last thing in the world I want to do. I need you, Shane. I've been feeling so alone, facing the decisions I have to make."

"If it helps, let me go on record saying that the pregnancy is something happening in your body, so that makes it your right to decide what to do about it. I'll back you up either way."

Merle lifted her head and looked up at him, studying the angle of his jaw, the way his hair had begun to recede at his temples, the generous shape of his nose, his caring eyes. It was the face of a strong man, a beloved man. The father of her— "Shane, I've been talking about making a decision, but I couldn't ever bear to—" She broke off, afraid to put her dream, her wish, her need into words. "I want this baby so desperately. Worse than you possibly could."

Relief washed through him. "Merry, darlin', I'm—"

She cut him off with her fingers on his lips. "It's too soon to let ourselves hope, much less get excited." Then, pulling away from his arms, she sat down and leaned her elbows on the table, rubbing her face wearily. "And we can't cancel out the option to terminate until after I've had an amniocentesis."

"Oh." His color had faded, leaving his tan a little grayish.

Merle peered at him. "What's the matter?"

He tried for a grin. "I know it sounds stupid, but I'm squeamish about needles and procedures and things like that. Too much time spent in hospitals, I guess."

Merle put her hand over his on the table. "You mean when you were wounded in the war? It must have been awful for you." Her eyes were questioning, wondering about the things that had shaped and formed the man he was.

To her surprise a flicker of anger stirred in his face, then he said tersely, "It was a long time ago and doesn't have anything to do with now."

She withdrew her hand. "Sorry, I didn't mean to pry."

"You weren't, it's just that . . ." He rasped his fingers over the roughness of his jaw, then shrugged the subject off. "When will you have this amniocentesis?"

"One o'clock tomorrow. Dr. Shapiro wants it done as soon as possible, in case we need to . . . you know."

He hesitated, but offered gamely, "Do you want me to come with you and stand by?"

Merle fought a battle with herself, wanting to say yes, that she wanted and needed him. But the queasy look on his face induced her to make a sacrifice for him. "Thanks for offering, love, but I'm a big girl now, I can cope with it on my own."

He looked apologetic but grateful. "Good thing you're a big girl, because I don't seem to be a very big boy. It's a sad state of affairs to be such a baby at forty-one that I can't hold your hand through a little needle."

"It isn't a little needle, it's a great big one," she said, then smiled at the expression on his face. Lord knew she had enough weaknesses of her own. The fact that Shane had one, too, made him more human, a little less bigger than life, as he sometimes seemed.

"Tell you what," she said, reaching out to clasp his hand, "you can pay penance by making dinner for me. Either your toast and jam or the talking—or both—has cured my nausea. I'm starving."

"You're on," he said, lifting her hand to his lips.

Eight

Dear Miss Merry,

I'm fifteen years old and I like to fantasize about the future. It's fun to imagine getting married someday. What do you think is the most important quality in a good husband?

Curious

Dear Curious

You're certainly looking ahead, aren't you, love? You've asked a difficult question, because there are so many important qualities one would hope for in a husband. But I'd have to say openness and sensitivity are most important in the long run. What woman wouldn't love to have a husband who cares enough to understand her needs?

Miss Merry

Merle stood outside the OB-GYN clinic, wearing a new outfit for the occasion, a loose yellow jumper over a figured blouse. She hoped it made her look chubby instead of pregnant, and that the sunny color would bolster her courage. She read and reread the list of five doctors printed on the door. Though Shapiro was a friend as well as her doctor, she felt butterflies the size of eagles fluttering in her stomach. It was fairly obvious why women generally had a husband in the wings before they went into pregnancy, because she felt very, very alone.

It was the baby she was frightened for, not herself. Now that Shane had forced her to admit she wanted the baby so very much, the disappointment would be crushing if the amniocentesis showed it—he? she?—wasn't perfect.

Shane. She wanted him so badly at this moment, his arms around her, his funny tongue taking the edge off her worry. The very thought of him sent a thrill of warmth spreading through her heart, her entire body. She no longer doubted it was love she felt. The wonder of it was that she felt certain he loved her too. She pondered the fact that he wanted the baby so badly too. Obviously he was a good, rare, special man.

So, if everything was so idealistic, she asked herself with something akin to despair, why couldn't they get along? Even at this very moment, though she understood why he wasn't with her today, she felt resentment over his absence eroding the warmth of love. It was a feeling she couldn't grasp much less control. And she knew there was so much he kept hidden. Why did they have to have such a combustible chemistry between them, sending them at each other's throats whenever they came together?

Thinking about their relationship was as upsetting and frightening as the amniocentesis, and it certainly didn't make her feel less alone. Taking a deep breath, she opened the door and walked into the clinic.

Surprise and almost giddy relief stopped her short just inside the door. Shane was sitting on a stiff chair, paging absently through a dog-eared magazine, looking very tall and broad-shouldered in a blue suit and paisley tie—and as out of place as the proverbial bull in the china closet, surrounded by a bevy of women in varying stages of pregnancy. When he noticed her at the door, he threw down the magazine and got up, pulling every gaze with him as he walked across the waiting room.

Grabbing his hand, Merle dragged him out into the corridor and shut the door. "What are you doing here?"

"I don't know, nothing better to do, I guess," he said with a grin, hiding his apprehension behind flippancy. "It occurred to me that yesterday I was pretty high-handed about insisting this is my pregnancy too. So, after spending the night wrestling with the devil and either winning or losing, depending upon your viewpoint, I decided I couldn't let you face the amniocentesis alone."

"Maybe you lost your bout with the devil, but I won." Burrowing into his arms, she pressed her face against his vested chest and went limp with relief. "I'm so glad you're here, I could cry. I'm so scared."

Holding her close, he rested his cheek on her head. "Everything is going to be all right, Merry."

"Oh, Shane, I wish I could be sure. I'd almost rather not know if there's something wrong with the baby."

He stroked her back and whispered in a put-on brogue, "Don't be lookin' for trouble before it finds you, darlin'. The Irish are fey, don't you know? Trust me, this Irishman has a feelin' everything is going to be just fine."

Lifting her head, she gave him a tremulous smile. "You're a perfect fake, but I want to believe you so badly, I will."

"I'm not a perfect anything," he said, grinning down at her.

"You're perfectly wonderful, that's what you are. You don't know how much I need you to hold my hand and cheer me on while they do the procedure."

"Hold your hand?" He swallowed convulsively, as if he'd been hit with more than he'd bargained for. "Surely they won't let me in while it's going on, will they?"

"Sure, that's what fathers are for." She looked up at him. He'd turned several degrees paler under his tan. "But I'll understand if it'll bother you too much. Just knowing you're in the waiting room is enough."

Shane looked into her huge dark eyes, then lowered his brows in determination. "If you can survive it, I ought to be able to. I'll hold your hand, darlin'."

She gladly gave in and put her hand in his as they walked into the clinic to present themselves at the desk.

Within half an hour Merle was lying on the treatment table. The air around her was filled with intimidating medical scents. A gowned nurse was standing by. The ultrasound technician was twiddling with her equipment.

Shane was sitting on a stool by Merle's head, wearing a green surgical gown over his clothes. He valiantly tried to keep her spirits up—or more likely his own—with some ridiculous patter about having always wanted to be young Dr. Kildare. She could feel him trembling and clasped his hand tighter.

Dr. Shapiro, a man in his fifties, walked into the room and smiled at Merle while putting on a gown and mask. "Hello there, young lady. Are you all ready for this?"

"As ready as I'll ever be, I guess," she answered, and lifted Shane's hand up. "This is Shane Halloran. He's my . . . uh . . . the significant other in all this."

Over the mask, the doctor's eyes showed surprise and curiosity, but all he said was, "Good to meet you, Shane. Significant others are always welcome here. You look a little shaky. Are you all right?"

Shane smiled and nodded. "Yeah, sure, I'm fine."

"Good. Let's get the show on the road, then."

The technician smeared a gel that felt like ice over

the mound low in Merle's belly, then ran her scanner slowly over it, making adjustments on the bank of knobs and dials. A blurred picture took form on a monitor.

"I'll be damned, look at that—after all these years it's still something to see," the doctor exclaimed, snapping surgical gloves on. "There he or she is. The baby's back is to us, so we can't tell which. We'll call him the generic 'he.'"

"Where?" All Merle could see was an incomprehensible blob on the monitor. "I can't make anything out."

The technician ran a forefinger over the picture. "Here he is, from here to here. There's the head, bent forward. This is his back, turned toward us, this is an elbow, and a knee here. Whoops, he's stretching out his legs."

Staring at the image on the monitor, Merle held her breath, her lips parted. A thrill as strong as an electric shock ran through her body when the little leg kicked out again; there really was a miniature human nestled in her body. A smile crept over her face. She glanced up and met Shane's gaze. "This isn't just a problem pregnancy, is it?"

"No, it isn't, that's our kid." He lit up the room with his grin and looked back at the monitor. "Did you see that, darlin'? There he goes again. Frisky little devil, isn't he?"

"Isn't he just!" She hoped it was a good sign.

Gasping over a wash of cold antiseptic on her belly, Merle turned her attention to the procedure. "All you're going to feel is a pinprick of local anesthetic," the doctor said. "After that takes effect, you won't feel a thing when I put in the bigger needle."

She felt the prick and numbing, and heard Shane make a funny sound in his throat. When she looked up at him, his face was the color of a honeydew melon and was beaded with sweat. His pupils were large enough to blot out the blue. "Shane, are you all right?" she asked anxiously.

"Right as rain," he whispered, slipping off the stool and out of sight.

The nurse and technician were accustomed to that sort of thing and caught him before he hit the floor, waving an acrid-smelling capsule under his nose. Then, one on each arm, the two women boosted him up on his wobbly legs and handed him out the door to the receptionist at the desk.

The rest of the procedure went textbook-perfectly. When it was over, Merle put on her cheerful jumper and blouse and went into the doctor's office to sit beside Shane in front of the desk. His tie was pulled loose and the top of his shirt was unbuttoned. "You scared me to death!" she said. "I thought you'd had a heart attack. Are you sure you're all right now?"

"Yes, I'm all right," he answered grumpily. "Except I feel like a fool."

She gave a laugh. "Why, Shane, love, I do believe your masculine ego got bruised when you took that nosedive."

Dr. Shapiro came in and went into a spiel of doctorly advice and orders, finishing up by asking Shane about his family background. "You're a twin, are you? Well, we saw only one little fellah in there, unless there was another one hiding around the corner. I'll call the minute we have the test results back from the lab, then we'll know what's going on. We should hear in about three weeks."

Merle felt her heart drop. "It takes that long? I could go out of my mind with worry in three weeks."

"Two at the very soonest, if I put a rush on it." He jotted a few words on the form. "Do you want to know the sex of the baby? It might make a difference in making a decision about whether to terminate or not."

Merle reached out and clasped Shane's hand. "I've—we've decided to go through with the pregnancy. At least we are if the baby is all right. The very least of my worries is whether it's a boy or a girl." She glanced at Shane. "Do you want to know?"

He shook his head. "No, I'd rather be surprised. It'll be like waiting for a Christmas present."

A few minutes later they left the clinic and rode down in the elevator. "Do you have your car today?" Shane asked when they were standing outside the building.

"No, I took a taxi."

A stubborn look settled on his face. "I'm going to drive you home. Don't argue with me."

Merle smiled angelically. "When do I ever argue? As a matter of fact, I'd appreciate a ride. I feel a little weak in the knees."

"Well, heaven be praised for minor miracles!" he exclaimed. "This is a first—she admits to being human."

"You better quit, or I'll change my mind and take the bus."

"Try it and I'll kidnap you."

"That might be exciting." She raised her brows. "We aren't talking about me hanging onto the back of your motorcycle, I hope."

"No, I came prepared, I've got my car. Wait here and I'll go get it."

He parked at the curb and solicitously belted Merle into the passenger seat, then slid behind the wheel and merged into the San Francisco rush-hour traffic on I-80. "Watching the sonograms was quite an experience, wasn't it?" he said, inching along with the slow-and-go traffic on the lower level of the Bay Bridge. "I'm glad I came. I wouldn't have missed seeing the baby for anything."

"It was thrilling, wasn't it?" Merle took the ultrasound picture out of her purse and studied the hazy image of her baby, awed by the fact that a new little life was growing inside her. Her face became tense with anxiety. "You don't think there could really be anything wrong with the baby, do you?"

He stared at the road, his forehead creased. "The sonograms showed two arms and two legs, so there's nothing obviously amiss. I doubt that he would've acted so frisky if there'd been a serious defect. That's what I think."

"Yes, I think so too," she said quickly, pathetically eager to be convinced.

The line of traffic stopped again, giving him a free moment to bend sideways and look at the picture. "Could you feel it when he kicked?"

She gave him a teasing look. "He? What makes you think it's a he? Do you have a chauvinistic urge to reproduce yourself?"

"Not particularly. One of me is probably all the world can handle. I was using Shapiro's generic 'he.'" Shane let out the clutch to inch forward with the rest of the gridlock mob. "All right, could you feel *her* kick?"

"No, I couldn't feel him, he must be too tiny yet." She laughed when he made a face at her, then went serious. "The odds must be very high against getting pregnant just like that, when we only made love two times on one day. It sounds like a fantasy of some sort. Too much of a coincidence to believe."

Shane gave a laugh. "If I'm not mistaken, that's a basic teenage misconception. That just that once couldn't possibly do any harm. Surely Miss Merry has had letters to that effect."

"Bushels." Merle smiled. "But we aren't teens, and I'm utterly dumbfounded that this could have happened. A mindless sperm cell from you and a brainless egg from me, drawn together like a couple of magnets. Now, like magic, there's a little peanut of a baby growing inside me."

"It's not magic," he said, exiting the bridge and lane-hopping to merge onto Highway 24. "It's a miracle."

"Yes, a miracle."

Merle put the picture away and turned her face toward the side window, thinking about the future as she stared at the tiled walls and emergency telephones inside the Caldecot Tunnel. "I'm scared," she said finally. "I'm not sure I'm capable of being a proper mother to a miracle."

"I can't think of anyone I'd rather have be a mother to my baby."

"But how am I going to know what's best for our little generic him? So many problems are bound to pop up. Like what on earth will I do if he *is* twins? And what's going to happen to Miss Merry? That's on top of the list, because how can I support a baby without a job?"

"We'll just have to play it by ear, darlin'. Don't be such a worrywart. Everything will work out, you'll see."

"I truly hope so." Merle lay back against the headrest and studied his profile through her lashes. His chin was solid, his nose aggressive, his shoulders straight and broad under the blue material of his suit. Everything about him exuded confidence, down to the knee jutting out as he worked the pedals with his foot, piloting the car down the off-ramp and onto the access road below her house.

She thought it odd for such a strong, capable, and self-confident man to faint over a simple medical injection. It wasn't a matter of courage, he had plenty of that or he wouldn't have been there in the first place. The years of his life in which she'd had no part had obviously left deep scars.

She reached out and curled her fingers around his thigh, then smiled when he glanced at her. "It was awfully brave of you to come and be with me today when you knew it would bother you. I'd like to be able to understand what happened back when you were in the war. Could you tell me a little about it?"

"Yeah, well . . ." He flexed his fingers on the wheel,

scowling through the windshield as he maneuvered up her driveway. Then he glanced at her, hiding behind a grin. "Look, it's hard enough on my tattered masculine ego for you to see me play the jerk and conk out, without having to go into the rest of the sordid story."

Merle jerked her hand back, feeling as if he'd slapped her interest and concern down.

Parking the car close to her house, Shane jumped out and ran around to take her arm. He led her into the house and settled her on a ruffled, cozy sofa in the living room, tucking pillows around her. "Can I get you anything?"

She waved him off, still feeling resentful. "Good grief, Shane, you're making me feel like an invalid."

"I was hoping to make you feel nurtured."

"You've succeeded, now enough's enough." Slipping off her shoes, she tucked her feet up and fussily arranged her sunny yellow skirts around her knees.

He sat down beside her, his chin up. "Hey, this is me, Shane, the father of the child you're carrying—remember? What's the matter, don't you trust me?"

She glanced up. "I expect I trust you just about as much as you trust me."

His blue eyes narrowed. "What do you mean by that?"

"You certainly weren't very eager to trust me when I expressed a concern about you and your fainting spell."

He slouched down on the sofa, stretched out his legs, crossed his feet, and shoved his hands in his trouser pockets. "That's entirely different."

"Oh, it is now? Then why are you closing down and shutting me out again?"

"I am not shutting you out," he said, then pulled himself upright. "I didn't realize I was, sorry. Look, I *can't* talk about those things, they just won't come out." His expression begged for understanding. "Someday, maybe, but not now."

She nodded, unsatisfied. "Okay. I imagine that's the answer I might give about trusting you too. Someday, maybe."

He studied her for a moment, then lifted her hand to his lips, kissing the knuckles. "We've got a long way to go yet, don't we?"

"Yes, I'm afraid so. She cocked her head. "But maybe there's hope. Do you realize we've just brushed up against some pretty heavy feelings without bickering about them?"

He glanced at her in surprise, then nodded. "It was a perfect opportunity for a spat, wasn't it? I wonder why we let it pass for a change?"

"Another minor miracle, I guess." She studied him, examining her own feelings. "You know something, Shane?"

"Hmm?"

"I think this day is the first time I've ever been with you without feeling an overwhelming urge for sex. It's kind of a relief."

He gave her a quick sidelong look, brows down. "Well, thanks a bunch, kiddo."

She laughed at his expression. "Your poor masculine ego is really taking a beating today, isn't it? But don't worry, the attraction is still there. I didn't mean to suggest you aren't still the sexiest man I've ever met."

"I should hope not." He laughed too. "But what are you getting at?"

"I don't know, I'm trying to think it through. All we've ever been to each other is lovers, and . . ." She played absently with an enameled earring, letting the sentence dangle, unsure of her point.

Shane finished for her. "And there has to be something more than sex to build a relationship on. You're saying our relationship is one-dimensional, and that's why we flare up and fight so easily." He licked his finger and touched her knee as if testing a hot iron. "I think you're saying that we generate enough sexual tension between us to set fires."

"I'm so glad you can read my mind, because you have a wonderful way with perspective," she said, laughing. "All I know is, if we're going to survive my pregnancy, never mind parenthood, we'd better learn how to be friends as well as lovers."

"I can't argue that point." He gave her a puckish grin and a questioning look. "But I hope you're not planning to cancel the other out entirely. I've always found our lovemaking to be fairly inspiring."

Dimples flickered at the corners of Merle's smile. "We created a little miracle, so our loving is made in heaven, right?"

"Absolutely, darlin'." Shane took her into his arms and hugged her.

Merle rested her head on his shoulder and sighed contentedly.

Suddenly all her anxiety came back and grabbed her like a vise. She tightened her arms and burrowed her face into the curve of his neck. "Shane, I don't think I can survive the disappointment if the amniocentesis results come back saying the baby isn't perfect."

"I'll have to admit this might be the longest three weeks known to the history of man." He held her, comforting her with his very presence, the rhythm of his breathing, the beat of his heart. "Our best bet is to stay busy and not leave time to think and worry."

Merle nodded, clinging to him. "What are you going to do to keep busy?"

"Oh, I don't know. For starters I think I'll stay here to make dinner and keep you company for the night." He quickly amended the offer. "As a friend not a lover, because no matter what happens with the test results, it's time for us to begin building a real relationship. What do you think?"

She lifted her head and smiled tremulously up at him. "I'd like that a lot."

Nine

Dear Miss Merry,
My boyfriend broke up with me and started dating my best friend. I'm pretending I don't care, but inside I hate them and the whole world. How can I quit thinking about how furious I am at both of them?

Steaming

Dear Steaming,
You mustn't bury the unresolved anger, my love. It will fester deep down inside. Talk about it to someone you trust: your mother, a counselor, a favorite teacher. But you must get rid of the anger before it sours the way you look at life and react to people.

Miss Merry

After the amniocentesis the days crept by for Merle, one after another. Fear of being caught with Shane by the media had sunk to the bottom of her priority list. To her eternal gratitude he called once or twice during every work day, always full of chatter about his frustrating, slow-moving trial.

Her nausea had passed, so in the evenings he took her to eat at out-of-the-way restaurants, and afterward to stage plays, concerts, and comedy clubs. Some nights they took turns cooking dinner at her place or on his houseboat.

There were no demands, no expectations, just a drawing together of two very anxious people who just happened to be in love. Desire was there, always, but they resisted, standing by their decision to put sensual needs on hold until they knew each other well enough to risk intimacy again.

By unspoken agreement they shied away from discussing emotionally combustive subjects, such as the baby and their common past. Instead they talked endlessly about neutral subjects: their work, friends, likes and dislikes, foods, vacations. At this stage they were being very careful, and it frightened Merle to suspect that only awareness and control kept them from bickering about their differences.

The closest they came to touching on their teen affair was to discuss Valerie Valerto. "Val and I had lunch today," Merle said on a Thursday evening as they were lingering over espresso in her sun-room. She was trying to thread a needle with pink embroidery floss to stitch a counted cross-stitch rose. "There wasn't any holding her off any longer, so I finally had to talk to her."

"How'd it go?" Shane dunked a sugar cookie in his coffee, then muttered under his breath when half of it disintegrated and fell in.

"Not as bad as I anticipated. Damn!" The double strand of floss bent, resisting the eye of the needle; she wet it in her mouth and tried again, one eye closed. "She was content with a surface review of how it was to have a baby out of wedlock and give her up, then how it felt to meet Ellen after so many years. She didn't asked about the lurid details."

"When's the article coming out?" he asked, staring into his coffee and chasing crumbs with his spoon.

"Not for a while, because she's thinking about talking to other people and professionals and expanding it into a series." The floss went through the eye finally. "She wants to talk to Ellen and you too."

"Me!" Shane glanced up from his fishing expedition. "Cripes, I'm scared to death of the woman. She's predatory."

Merle laughed, her eyes inches from the minuscule pattern as she inserted the needle. "Val's nothing but a big actress. Even if she weren't, I rather imagine the two of you are fairly well matched." She pulled the pink thread through the material and glanced up, smiling. "You put on a pretty good act yourself yesterday, staging a sit-in on the steps of that empty warehouse with your young female clients."

His smile was humorless.

Merle brushed the hair off her forehead with her wrist, holding the needle in her fingers. "I'm curious—are they as interested in getting themselves off the street as you are?"

He began fishing for crumbs again. "A few of them are, too few—but if I can salvage even one or two, I consider them worth my effort. The rest go along with me because sometimes I give them a chance to thumb their noses at the cops." He grinned. "If I don't accomplish anything else, I'm always good for a few laughs."

"I'll agree with them about that," she said, making the second cross. "What came of your sit-in?"

"The city claims the warehouse is impractical as a safe house because it's in the wrong area and too expensive to remodel. But that's hogwash." He gave up on the spoon and sipped his coffee, crumbs and all.

The floss slipped out of the needle on the third cross, and Merle impatiently threw the whole business down. "Are you giving up on the idea, then?"

His brows shot up in surprise. "I never give up on

anything, Merry. Haven't you figured that out yet? I've only just begun to fight."

On the fifteenth night after the amniocentesis they were sitting on the deck of the houseboat, listening to folk music from the stereo accented by the slap of waves. Merle, dressed in new, bigger jeans and one of Shane's shirts, was trying not to worry as she lay on a padded lounger, staring up at the stars. Her loose, wavy hair gleamed platinum in the faint light. "Oh, did Ellen call you?" she asked. "She came back from her honeymoon today."

"Did she ever—happy and replete after bumming around Germany on the trains for two weeks." Shane, stretched out on a lounger beside her, flung one leg over the other and gave a laugh. "You'd told her about little Oops by the time she talked to me, but I thought she took the news rather philosophically."

"Yes, she did." Merle smiled over her daughter's reaction. "Let me quote verbatim: 'How on earth could that have happened? But then nothing goes by plan between you and Shane, does it—so where'd I come from? How funny to think I'm going to have a full-blooded brother or sister.'"

He laughed again. "Bless her for being tolerant of her elders."

Merle turned her head and looked at him. "You're a man, so maybe she didn't tell you. She intended to come back pregnant from her honeymoon, but got her period instead. She's upset because she'd scheduled a baby for nine months after marriage."

"Poor darlin'," Shane commiserated. "We all have our problems, don't we?"

Merle picked up a glass of fruit juice and took a sip, then rested the glass on the rapidly expanding mound under her jeans. "Her reaction to Valerie and the article surprised me. She thinks it'll be exciting to be interviewed by a reporter. You don't suppose your family is rubbing off on her, do you?"

"Oh, cripes, not Halloran pollution." Shane groaned, and then he said, "I can hardly remember what life was ike before Ellen."

"Me either—she's my wish come true." Merle reached out to poke a knuckle at his upper arm. "Though I'll have to admit life was a lot simpler before, since she came as a package deal including you."

"Thanks a lot," he said, poking her back. "She's made me think a lot about being a parent. I have a feeling it isn't as simple as my folks made it look."

Somewhere in the dark at the edge of the pier, gulls fluttered and squawked, squabbling over space ights on posts, then quieted again. When Merle didn't comment, Shane peered at her through the darkness. "You never mention your parents—are hey still living in the Bay Area?"

She shifted uneasily on the cushioned lounger, pulling up her knees. "No. My father was promoted to president of his company's Brazilian division several years ago. They live in South America."

Waves splatted against the sides of the boat for several seconds while Shane gazed questioningly at her. Then he stepped over their ban on speaking of he past. "It seems to me I remember your parents reating you like little Miss Princess, the center of heir universe, when you were a kid. But now you sound as if you're talking about strangers."

A wave of loneliness flushed through her system. "We haven't been close since Ellen was born. I guess never really forgave them for railroading me into the adoption. Oh, we're polite enough—exchange letters occasionally, see each other once a year. But that's it." She clenched her hands on the lounger armrests. "What can I say? I had one life before you came along, Shane, and a very different life after."

He reached out to clasp his fingers around her clenched hand. "It's hard for me to understand there still being hard feelings after twenty-three years. My folks would have straightened me out quick enough."

Merle sat up and put her feet squarely on the deck, frowning in the darkness. Sometimes she missed them so much, needed them. But how did one make a new start after such a long time? "There's a world of difference between your parents and mine. Yours are happy you grew up without landing in jail. Mine had such high expectations, I couldn't live up to them." She patted her belly. "And I probably never will at the rate I'm going."

He swung his long legs off the lounger and sat up, facing her with his knees brushing hers. "Is that why you started dating me back then, Merry? Was it a rebellion against them?"

There was so much about her feelings for him that she didn't understand, the confusion of yearning, resentment, love, anger, and all the rest. "Oh, who knows why a sixteen-year-old does anything?" she said irritably, and stood up. "It's time for me to go home now. I'm all talked out for the night."

Later, after Merle had gone to bed, she wished she'd stayed. It would have been less agonizing to debate the motivations behind her problems with Shane than to lie awake worrying about the baby.

It was two-fifteen P.M. the next day before Shane finally returned Merle's call and had the audacity to ask, "Were you looking for me?"

She could have cheerfully strangled him. "Yes, I've been looking for you! Why didn't you answer your pager? Dr. Shapiro called me this morning with the results of the amniocentesis."

A few beats of silence. "And . . . ?"

"Everything tested out perfectly normal. Oh, Shane, the baby's all right!"

"Thank God!" He cleared his throat when his voice caught. "Listen, I've got a couple hour's worth of time spend here at court yet, but then I'll be free. I'll pick ou up at your office, and we'll celebrate, okay?"

"That sounds wonderful. But I'm no good for anying at work, so I'm going home. Come there."

Merle felt utterly emptied of anxiety about the baby, oating on happiness as she left the office. On npulse she popped into a downtown maternity shop buy a dress, just because there was a future for her regnancy.

Later, after she got home, she threw her clothes off nd stood in the shower hugging her belly, laughing nd talking aloud to the baby. She felt alive and oung as a kid, free, fulfilled. Hopping out again, she weled herself dry and blew her pale hair into a oud of soft, free waves brushing her shoulders.

Smiling, she touched a musky perfume to her neck nd breasts. As the months went by, she would illingly expand into a shapeless queen bee, but this ne last time she wanted to be attractive and desirble for Shane. She pulled on one of her dressier resses and peered critically in the mirror. Forget esirable: She looked as if she were smuggling a intaloupe under her skirt.

Bowing to the inevitable, she took the new materity dress out of the bag. It was an orange, white, nd yellow striped jersey with a low, round neck and tful gathers over the front. She put it on and irned this way and that in front of the mirror. It idn't look too bad with yellow flats and jewelry, but iere wasn't much danger of her knocking Shane ead in it.

Oh well, she decided philosophically, bending over pick up the clothes she'd thrown around, at least was a relief to have breathing space.

She waited impatiently at the window until she iw the headlight on Shane's motorcycle nosing off ie freeway onto the access road, and stood outside ie door as he weaved and swayed up her driveway. A reat surge of tenderness swept through her as she

watched him dismount in front of the house, hi
leather jacket thrown on over his gray suit pants an
white shirt, his tie pulled loose. He took off hi
helmet, revealing his mass of silver-black curl
Whatever their problems, she loved him to the depth
of her soul. This man, the father of her baby.

A toothy grin spread across his face when he sa
Merle standing on the stoop. Swiveling his hips, h
drove both fists up at the blue sky, letting out a yel
A flock of starlings exploded off the field below he
house. "He's okay, darlin'!" he called out when sh
ran toward him. "Ain't that something? It's real, it
going to happen."

He grabbed her up in his arms and whirled he
around. Her heart took wing, her body sparked to li
the instant he touched her. She threw her arm
around his neck, laughing with sheer joy. "Put m
down, you idiot!"

Setting her on her feet, he held her away by th
hands, grinning. "Look at you, Merry, all dressed u
in a sack."

"Don't you dare make fun of me, Shane Halloran
She laughed, too, and halfheartedly tried to pull he
hands free.

"I'm not making fun of you. I love it." He pulled he
back into his arms and pressed her against his bod

Then his laughing grin softened into a differer
kind of teasing smile. His blue eyes turned hot an
heavy. Bending his head, he rained tender fleetin
kisses on her cheeks, her eyelids, her neck. Sh
moaned softly, her skin burning. Desire explode
into full bloom. There was no sense to it, just a
overpowering need. Any previous resolutions to pos
pone sex evaporated.

When he moved his hands down her back to pres
her lower body against his, she felt his erectio
against her rounded belly. "What is this?" she aske
eyes shining. "Lusting over a pregnant woman in
sack? You must really be hard up."

Shane groaned. "You should be ashamed of yourself for mouthing such a pathetic pun. As you can very well feel, I am extremely hard up. After all, it's been almost five months since we made love, darlin'. Do you want to know how many weeks and days? Minutes?"

"I know exactly how long it's been, my sweet." She touched his lower lip with her finger. "Is that the truth? Haven't you had anyone else since then?"

"Cross my heart, all I want is you. Any other woman could parade naked and not get a rise out of me." He grinned down at her when *she* groaned this time. "Sack or no sack, Merry darlin', you drive me crazy. Just you, no one else."

Covering her lips with his, he nibbled and teased, and stepped forward, moving her legs backward in something like a dance step. When they were inside the house, he kicked the door shut behind them, closing the world out.

Any disinclination Merle might have felt for a tawdry affair evaporated when she slipped her arms under his jacket, running her hands over the layered muscles of his back. She stepped onto the tops of his large polished black shoes, and the dance step continued. He carried them both down the hallway, his thighs making love to hers in the motion of walking.

In her bedroom he held her hands. "Oh, Merry, my Merry, I've missed you so—this way."

"My darling, so have I. Welcome home."

He slid his tongue in her mouth, sending sensations racing through her body, driving her wild. His face was flushed when he lifted his head again. "I've been dreaming of this ever since the end of March."

She took his face between her two hands, the roughness of his afternoon beard tantalizing her palms. "It's been forever."

Reaching down, he ran his hands caressingly up her outer thighs, under her dress. She pulled back, suddenly shy. "Shane, I'm not the same as I was.

Pregnancy isn't the prettiest condition. Are you sure you won't be turned off by me now?"

"I can't imagine it," he murmured, his breathing heavy. "But how would I know? I haven't seen you yet." He ran his hands up her body, pushing the dress over her head, and let it fall.

The flickering blue flame of his eyes awakened every cell when he looked down at her breasts in a lacy pale yellow bra, at her swollen belly, her thighs, and the patch of yellow lace panties between. "Merry, heart o' mine, I've never seen you look so lovely, so soft and sweet." Then he gave a perfectly satyrish grin and cradled her breasts. "But you're right, you have changed. There's more of you than there used to be. Look how you fill my hands, darlin'. What's not to like about pregnancy? Even when you're nine months along, you'll torment me."

He made everything seem so natural and good that she laughed, melting with relief. "Better take advantage of them before they deflate again."

"You don't have to tell me twice." He slowly, slowly undressed her, kissing her skin as her wispy underthings fell, bringing a cry out of her when he touched his mouth to her taut, swollen nipples. Then he looked into her face, his lopsided grin teasing. "I'm not perfect either, Merry. Maybe when you take a look you won't want me."

"No!" she cried out as he lit fire to the soft parts of her body with his hands. "I mean, yes, oh, yes, I want you. I need you, my sweet."

Hands trembling, she pushed his leather jacket off to drop on the floor, his shirt following. She kissed the crisp hair and flat nipples on his chest as she frantically worked at his zipper and pants.

Lifting her onto the ruffled, flowered coverlet of her bed, Shane lay down beside her, smiling, tracing circles over her body with his finger. His smile wavered when he rested the flat of his hand around he swell above her blond pubic hair. "It won't hurt he baby if we make love, will it?"

She smiled. "I don't think so, it should be like ocking the cradle."

With that his desire became urgent. He touched ıer with the same demanding fingers and lips she'd ılways known, but there was a new awareness about ıim, a gentleness. After he'd brought her to full eadiness, he lifted her on top of his body and ntered her from below, then lay still, filling her, urning the lead over to her. Savoring the oneness, he held him in her arms, her face pressed into the urve of his neck. All the problems still lying before hem were pushed from her mind.

After a time she began to move, and he met her hythm, slowly at first and then without restraint. inally they lay quietly, limbs entwined, her slender eg flung over his scarred one. They were sweaty and eplete, clinging to the ecstatic, transitory oneness hey'd shared.

"I love you so much, Merry," Shane whispered ıgainst her ear.

"I love you, too, my darling."

Lying on her back, Merle nestled her cheek against ıis muscular shoulder. His lips moved on her fore-ıead. "No one can give me the joy that you do, heart ' mine."

"Joy . . ." She sighed.

With caressing fingers, he mapped out the familiar erritory of her body. He cupped his hand around the nound in her abdomen and held it there for a few noments. Suddenly he heaved up on an elbow, his xpression surprised. "Was that him I felt moving in here, Merry? Like a bird fluttering against my ıand? Did you feel it too?"

"I think so. Yes. It's the first time." Tears blurred ıer eyes. "Oh, Shane, now we know for sure the baby s all right."

He nodded, smiling down at her. Then he leaned

forward over her body and said softly. "Hullo in there little one. You know your mom pretty well, now it's time to get to know your daddy too. That was me bouncing you around a minute ago, in case you wondered."

Merle ran her fingers into his curly hair and tightened a fist, pulling him back down again "Shame on you! What a way to talk in front of an innocent child."

He laughed and kissed her. "I am what I am, and I'm too old to change, so he might as well get used to me early on."

She smiled. "Someday *she* might have a little trouble explaining to her kindergarten class why her mommy and daddy lock their bedroom door."

He touched her nose with the tip of a finger "Maybe, but Miss Merry can always explain everything to her."

"Miss Merry?" Merle turned her face toward his chest, closing her eyes against the rasp of crisp black hair. "I'm afraid Miss Merry is soon going to be in deep trouble. I can't hide my *flagrante delicto* condition much longer. The board of *Youngest Sister* will probably exile me to the basement to do grunt writing."

Shane slipped his fingers under her chin and lifted her head. "Oh, come on, darlin'! A single parent isn't that shocking in these modern times. Especially not here in the San Francisco Bay Area."

"Do you really think they'll accept it?" She looked into his eyes, desperate to believe he had some knowledge that she hadn't considered yet.

"I know so, trust me," he said without the slightest doubt in his voice. "It makes better sense to worry about, oh, say, salting away a college fund. Tuition at Yale is going to be out of sight in eighteen years."

She scowled, her eyes sparkling. "Good Lord Shane, Yale? I suppose the first thing you did when you heard I was pregnant was enroll her in a yuppie nursery school, so she'll have a spot waiting for her at age three."

"Nah, if he goes to one of those, he might grow up ashamed of me."

She laughed. "It'd make more sense if you'd offer to help me decorate a nursery for her."

"Her," he repeated, sighing. "Are we going to do the nursery in pink?"

"Him. No, I don't think pink would do. We'd better play it safe and do it up in a nice generic pastel color."

They lay quietly for a time, then Shane walked his fingers up her arm, tickling. "Are you ready to do the job up right yet, darlin'? Let's get married—signed, sealed, and stamped." His lopsided grin spread across his face. "It'd solve a lot of stray problems if we make it legal. I'll make an honest woman of you, then your reputation and Miss Merry will be safe."

Her heart leaped with yearning—and then anxiety when she searched his face, only to find his serious feelings shuttered away by his grin. "We're a little old for a shotgun wedding, aren't we?" she asked cautiously.

He gave her belly a teasing pat. "If we aren't too old for the cause, we shouldn't be too old for the effect."

His bantering began to wear on her. "Shane, don't joke about something so serious as marriage. You don't have to marry me just because I'm pregnant. Didn't you say single parenting is in?"

"What makes you think I'm joking?" he asked defensively. "It seems only appropriate to discuss marriage at a time like this. You can't disagree with that, can you?"

"Of course not! It's the way you're going at it that bothers me." Merle snapped her mouth shut and closed her eyes, wondering why they couldn't ever discuss their feelings without both of them tightening up like rubber bands. "Oh, Shane, I wish . . ."

For the moon, the stars, the impossible.

"I'll make all your wishes come true, darlin'," he promised expansively. "What do you wish?"

Turning on her side, she cuddled against him and put her arm over his chest. "I wish we were starting out all new," she said fervently. "I wish we could erase everything that went before. You know what I mean, we've talked about this before. Neither one of us has a very good track record in relationships."

"Yes, I know." He cupped his hand around her cheek. "But think about it, Merry, we've been behaving ourselves lately. We haven't had a fight in a month. That bodes well for working things out."

"I don't see us working things out at all. It's been less than a month since we fought, it's more like two weeks."

"Two weeks! No way." Shane pulled himself up and swung his long legs off the bed.

"Has too." She got out of bed and picked up her clothes, holding them balled against her breasts as she stalked toward the bathroom.

"Okay, refresh me," he demanded, following on her heels with a defiant limp. "What did we fight about two weeks ago?"

"Day before the amniocentesis we fought about whether I should or shouldn't terminate." She stepped into the large shower stall and closed the glass door rather loudly.

He pulled it open and followed her in, his tall, broad-shouldered body seriously crowding the space. "For cripes' sake, what kind of a steel-trap memory do you have?"

"One that compensates for your convenient amnesia." She turned on the water, gritting her teeth against the cold.

Yelping, he backed out of the icy needles of water. "Wait a minute, the amniocentesis was more than two weeks ago. You look on the calendar, and you'll see it's closer to three weeks ago. We've been together

t least part of every day for almost three weeks and
ot one fight. Does your memory concede to that?"
The water turned warm. Merle let out the breath
he'd been holding and said grudgingly, "I'll concede
o the surface truth."
She wet herself all over, then watched Shane step
nto the spray while she stood back and soaped with
perfumed bar. The scars on his right leg were a
ivid reminder that he'd locked her out of a large slice
f his life, and away from himself. "Well, it seems to
ne we've had to work hard at maintaining our
mnesty," she said irritably. "The urge to fight is
lways there, ready to flare up, and it isn't good
nough to control it with willpower."
He ducked his head under the spray, flattening his
air against his head, and scowled darkly through
he streaming water. "You're just dreaming up trou-
le now."
"I am not, I'm being realistic!" She angrily soaped
er face with her hands, then groped blindly toward
im. "I've got soap in my eyes! Let me get under the
hower!"
Guiding her under the spray, Shane held her chin
p to wipe her eyes with a washcloth. She blinked
er vision clear and slapped the bar of soap into his
and. "I'm not dreaming up trouble! We were on the
erge of fighting a dozens times in these last couple
f weeks."
"Name one," he challenged, running the gardenia-
cented soap over his underarms and chest.
It made her even more angry that she couldn't
hink of one off the top of her head. "I can't remem-
er, but that doesn't mean there weren't any." She
vatched with narrowed eyes as he rinsed himself
vith a furious spattering of water. "How about right
ow for example? I'd say our voices are raised pretty
igh over whether we do or don't fight."
Shane stood motionless for a few moments, the
pray running in rivulets down over his torso and

legs, realization twisting his face. "Oh, cripes, why now of all times? Just when everything was so good—the baby, the lovemaking. What *is* this bickering of ours all about? Why?"

"I wish I knew. Let's face it, Shane, we're a disaster waiting to happen." Turning unhappily, she stepped out of the shower and wrapped a peach-colored towel around her head, and another oversize one around her body as if for protection.

Shane turned off the spray and came out to wrap a towel around his waist. "Much as I hate to admit it, your point is valid," he said in a low voice, his face troubled. "Obviously we're never more than a hair trigger away from a lightning storm."

"Yes, I'm afraid so. And the point I've been trying to make is, if we're bickering during courtship, if that's what this is, then what kind of war would we carry on if we got married?" Merle rubbed her fingertip on his forearm, ruffling up the short black hairs. "It'd be terrible to get married for our little defenseless baby's sake, then subject him to our fighting, or worse to divorce."

Shane opened his arms and she went into them. They held each other with quiet desperation for a time. Then Shane said miserably, "I feel as if I'm beating my head against a brick wall. It's three feet thick and ten feet tall, and it's keeping us apart."

She pressed her face wearily into his broad shoulder. "You asked what I wished for? I know now. I wish, I *wish* we could find some way to climb over the stupid wall."

Ten

Dear Miss Merry,
I'm writing back to tell you I went to the counseling center and they did a pregnancy test. It came out positive. How could something so awful happen to me? They say I should tell the boy and my parents. But I'm too embarrassed and scared. Please write and tell me if there is some way to make a go of it on my own.

Cindy Jones

My dear Cindy,
Darling, please, please, don't try to handle this alone. The boy should be told, because he is equally responsible. But if you can't tell him, do tell your parents immediately. Trust me, they will understand, give you emotional support, and help you decide what to do about the pregnancy. If you try to do this alone, you won't have the financial means to live, pay doctor bills, or. . . .

Valerie Valerto kicked off her series about adoption in the *San Francisco Chronicle* on the last Sunday of

August. Her first article featured Merle's relationship with Ellen and Shane Halloran.

Late in the afternoon of the Wednesday after, Merle dropped in unannounced on Shane at his office. "You busy?" she asked.

Obviously he was, sitting behind his big desk with a mountain of paperwork in front of him. He had his jacket off, his vest unbuttoned, his tie yanked loose, and his shirtsleeves rolled up. "I'm never too busy for you, Merry, darlin'," he said, stretching his fists over his head. His spine bowed with a series of creaks. "To what do I owe this unexpected but very welcome surprise?"

"Nothing, I just felt like talking." She sat down on the sofa by the window and pulled her loose suit jacket around her body, concealing the rubber band and paper clip holding her skirt band together. "How is your day going?" she asked, putting off the subject so heavy on her mind.

He propped his crossed feet up on the corner of his desk and laced his fingers behind his head. "Frustrating as hell. I'll be lucky if Linda and I aren't laughed out of court when Hollbrook and his lawyers get done with us. I'm planning a little demonstration to make use of the publicity before we're shot down." He smiled wryly at her. "That's my day, how did yours go?"

"Fine." She morosely leaned her elbow on the sofa arm and her dimpled chin on the heel of her hand. "Except that I've been fired."

Shane stared for a second, mouth gaping. "You're joking! No, you don't joke about things like that." He dropped his feet to the floor with a clunk and came across the office to sit beside her. "What happened?"

"My editor in chief made an appointment for today to discuss the implications of Valerie's article. A quorum from the board of directors turned up, too, none of them under the age of sixty, and not one of them receptive to alternative lifestyles."

He frowned with disbelief. "But the article was about the psychology of adoption and reuniting biological parents and children. Valerie didn't go into any personal details."

"They would have accepted my having given up a baby for adoption, but not that I am pregnant again. I had to tell them, I can't hide it any longer." Merle pressed her hands over the bulge under her skirt, then got up to stand at the window. The setting sun had kindled a blaze on a long, stringy cloud that was sinking into the ocean—a fairly accurate reflection of her life at this point.

She looked back at Shane and stretched her lips into a sick smile. "It seems a woman who accidentally gets pregnant at age thirty-nine doesn't have any business giving advice to teenage girls. So says the board of *Youngest Sister.*"

Shane jumped up to stand beside her, taking her hands in his. "What an idiotic crock of—" He finished the sentiment under his breath.

"Oh, it's not, really. I can't say that I blame them. Much as I want the baby, it was pretty stupid of me to let it happen the way it did. I already knew the board didn't like the way I handle my column and suspected they were looking for an excuse to phase me out."

Merle had taken pride in not crying so far, but now her lower lip trembled when she said, "They asked my assistant to take over the column. I guess I'd rather she do it than some stranger, but she'll have to dig up a new name for it. Miss Merry is copyrighted to me, and I'd rather bury her than give her away."

Her control crumpled. "Shane, I've been Miss Merry for fifteen years. I feel as if someone has chopped off a big chunk of me."

"Aw, darlin', I'm so sorry. Come here, come to Papa." Shane gathered her into his arms, patting, stroking, murmuring comfort. When she'd cried it out, he handed her a large white handkerchief and frowned speculatively as she wiped her face and eyes and blew her nose. "A thing like that shouldn't have happened in this modern world. Why don't you bring suit against them for discrimination?"

Merle wrapped her arms around her body and began pacing. "What's the point? They'd never admit to retiring me because I'm pregnant. They'd say I didn't fit into the new, more conservative format for *Youngest Sister.*"

Shane paced at her side. "Give me a break, any lawyer worth his salt could get around that. Let me give it a try."

Stopping short, she turned on him. "Surely you can't picture me taking you on as a lawyer and making myself a target for even more media interest?"

His brows came down. "For cripes' sake, you aren't *still* worried about your precious reputation, are you?"

Her chin came up. "I've got a right to a reputation if I want one!" Taking a deep breath, she wrestled her temper down. "Shane, having our baby is a special, very private thing. I don't want it turned into a three-ring circus."

He rubbed his hand over his jaw and across his mouth. "Why didn't you say so first off, darlin'? That's something I can understand."

"Because you got up on your high horse so fast, I didn't have a chance."

He winced. "It seems like all I ever do is apologize, but one more time—I'm sorry. Come and sit down. Would you like a soda or some juice?"

"Juice, please." She perched on the edge of the sofa, waiting while he went to a mini-bar and poured tangerine juice over ice cubes in a tall glass. She took it and exclaimed, "What am I going to do, Shane? Nobody will hire a pregnant lady. How am I going to live? My house payments will eat my savings for a snack. And how can I pay for the baby without medical insurance?"

"Whoa. Wait just a minute here!" he said, planting himself in front of her. "Remember me? The financially responsible father? You can move in with me, if you want to. Or I'll move in with you—your house is the better choice for a family and children. Whichever, I'll pay the bills and take care of you."

Merle glanced up at him, taking a sip of juice and very precisely setting the glass on the coffee table, centering it. "It's sweet of you to offer, love, but we aren't ready for that yet. We'd be at each other's throats in a minute."

He looked at her impatiently, his lips parted as if he wanted to argue, but then he thought better of it. "Okay, how about it if I set up a bank account for you?"

"I truly appreciate your offer, Shane. But—" She slammed her fist down on the sofa arm. "But I've been on my own since I was sixteen years old, and I hate being so helpless! I don't want to depend on *anyone*. I want to be Miss Merry! What am I going to do with my days and weeks and months of pregnancy without a job? I'll go nuts!"

He sat down beside her and put his arm around her shoulders. "Darlin', it's not that long, and after the baby comes, you'll have plenty to keep you occupied."

"After the baby comes, I'll need a job even more than I do now." Picking up her glass, she jumped up and stood at the window, absently rattling the ice cubes. "It'll take time and energy to find a new job, not to mention carving out another niche for myself. How can I do justice to a baby at the same time?"

Shane sat forward on the sofa, elbows on his knees, hands clasped under his chin, watching her. "Okay, let's brainstorm this through. Don't forget I intend to take turns with the baby."

Merle frowned at him, pressing the icy glass to her cheek. Frustration spurred her to quibble somewhat unreasonably. "Where would *you* find time to meet the needs of a baby with all your rather peculiar interests?"

"You don't know the Halloran family very well, do you? Every woman is a mother at heart. They'd help us out."

Her eyes narrowed, a mother lioness again; she didn't want anyone taking her baby. "But that'd mean shuffling her back and forth between anyone who might be available. I firmly believe babies need a stable family and continuity. I'm beginning to wonder if it was selfish for me to want to keep this little one."

Shane unclasped his hands and hitched himself forward on the sofa. "What exactly are you trying to tell me, Merry."

"Nothing. I'm just trying to figure out how to give this precious little one growing in me the best possible life." She stared down into her glass, swirling the ice cubes around, rambling, talking through her insecurities. "Despite our troubles, I grew up in a nice, stable, two-parent family. You did too. I'm wondering if it's selfish to cheat our baby out of that kind of stability."

He let out an exasperated snort. "There are two of us, a mother and a father. He won't mind the shuffling as long as there's always someone around to love him."

Merle stared through the window. Traffic was rushing on the street below, while in the distance the ocean was peace incarnate. "Ellen told me I gave her two precious gifts—her life and parents who brought her up with a nice balance of guidance, love, and fun. If I were really unselfish, I would give this baby the same gifts."

Shane came off the sofa like a shot, his face dark, his eyes narrowed. Grasping her upper arms, he forced her to face him. "You just try giving this baby away, Merry! You just try it, and I'll fight you up to the highest court in the land."

"For heaven's sake, calm down!" Merle said, peeling his fingers off her arm. "You know perfectly well I wouldn't give up my baby unless there wasn't a single other solution. But I'm in a pickle just now, and the best choice for the future probably isn't the decision I've made to keep him. I'm just trying to talk away my guilt."

He studied her for a second longer, then rubbed his hand over the back of his neck. "Well, don't scare me like that."

"What do you expect when I've been strung up on wires since March?"

Standing side by side, they looked out at the sunset, Shane jingling change in his pockets, Merle rubbing one fingertip anxiously over the dimple in her chin.

After a few minutes he broke the silence. "If you need money before you get another job, I'll float you a loan. Even charge you interest, if that'd make you feel better. Would you consider that?"

"A loan? Yes, of course I'd accept a loan. Thanks." She glanced up at him. A smile dimpled the corners of her lips. "But be darned if I'll pay you interest."

His grin lit up his face. "Whatever you say, and thank goodness! That's one less thing to fight about."

Merle sighed. "It seems as if we should run out of topics to bicker over pretty soon, wouldn't you think?"

"What do you know about Lamaze, Bren?" Shane asked in the middle of September. He was sitting beside his twin sister, legs hanging free six feet above the ground on the top row of a set of mini-bleachers. They were watching ten-year-old Daniel junior play in an elementary school baseball game. The opposing team was at bat. Danny was playing left field.

"Enough to rewrite the book after giving birth to

three babies, I expect," she answered. "Why are you asking?"

"Merry's scheduled to start taking Lamaze classes in a month or so, when she's seven months along." He took the straw out and tipped up his paper glass for the last few drops of soda. Ice cubes tumbled down on his nose. "She asked me if I could handle being her coach. What's the coach do?"

Bren groaned when a fielder, not Danny, bobbled the ball and let the opposing batter get on first base. "The coach is supposed to talk his mate out of panicking, which causes pain, and into rhythmic breathing and relaxation." She grinned at him. "And when the going gets tough and his mate begins snarling, 'You did this to me, you bastard,' he gets to feel guilty."

"Thanks a lot, I needed that." Scowling, he worried the straw between his teeth, talking around it. "If, in your arcane way, you're telling me my place is beside Merry while she's in labor, I already know that. I want to do it. Just tell me *how*, with the way I am about hospitals. I won't be any good to her if I'm flat on my back."

His twin looked at him sympathetically. "I forgot about that phobia of yours. You've got a real problem, haven't you?" She waved her arms and cheered when the first baseman nabbed a weak line drive and threw the batter out. A minute later she winced when the next batter hit a drive which neatly threaded its way between the legs of the pitcher, the second baseman, and the shortstop.

Shane chewed on the straw, wondering what to do about the Lamaze problem; how would Merry take it if he couldn't be with her at the end? He spit out a paper shred when the straw disintegrated, and tipped up his glass for an ice cube to suck instead.

It was frustrating, the way he and Merry always seemed to be circling around each other instead of drawing together—like the disagreement they had over her financial problems. It was a major issue, not just bickering, and worse, they hadn't truly resolved it. At least not to his satisfaction.

He'd taken enough psychology courses in college to know something subconscious in both of them was causing their relationship to be fragile and tenuous at best.

Bren gave a raucous yell when Danny caught a line drive, bobbled it, tripped over his own feet, and made it to the base for the out anyway. "That's my boy! Did you see that?"

"See what?" Shane asked.

"Are you living in a parallel universe or what?" Bren aimed a clout at his shoulder. "And about Lamaze, answer me this one—if Merry was the one phobic about hospitals, she couldn't beg out of the labor and delivery, could she?"

He shook his head. "I guess she couldn't."

"Then you'd better either desensitize yourself or be awfully damned open about why you can't be there when *your* baby is born. One or the other."

Eleven

Dear Miss Merry,

I was fourteen when you first began writing your column, and you were such an important part of my life. I was shocked and heartbroken when I read in the Chronicle *that you won't be doing your column any longer. I have a little girl of my own now, and how on earth can she grow up without Miss Merry to guide her? It doesn't matter what happened in your personal life, as long as you understand girls who are searching for maturity. Or perhaps it matters a great deal, because your experiences have made you all the better at what you do. Please come back, Miss Merry. No one can take your place.*

(Mrs.) Marilyn Corbet

By the end of October the hills had turned golden and the pin oak trees around Merle's house had taken on the rust color of autumn. She was into her seventh month, trying to keep busy with a healthy regime of diet, exercise, and doctor's appointments.

She'd begun writing the book about relationships in the teen years, but her heart wasn't in it. She was still in mourning for Miss Merry, silly as it seemed.

It was her salvation that Shane spent most of his free time with her. Their relationship had slipped into an uneasy, frustrating peace. They didn't fight, but neither did they discuss their feelings. Still, he did make her laugh, and boosted her spirits by helping decorate the nursery with a cunning baby wallpaper and choosing infant clothes and furniture.

On the last Friday afternoon in October Merle put on a turquoise maternity exercise suit with white stripes down the sleeves and legs. She carried two pillows in a duffel bag onto the BART train, heading for an early dinner with Shane, and after that to her first Lamaze class. She hoped the classes would erase the somewhat excessive, very annoying fear of labor and delivery she'd begun to suffer lately.

Shane was waiting outside Riley's Place in his biker boots and leather jacket. His grin was cocky and his curly silver-black hair tousled. She imagined he'd make quite a splash at a birthing class. "Hullo, darlin'," he said, putting his arms around her, pillows and all. He kissed her on the lips, then looked teasingly down at her. "Have you been behaving yourself today? Did you exercise the way you're supposed to? Take your vitamins? Watch your weight? Stay away from the cookies and ice cream?"

Rather than admit to indulging in the latter, she asked, "How would you like a good karate kick?"

"Not particularly, though it might be interesting to see you try in your shape." He held the door open with an arm, a big grin lighting his face.

"Keep it up, buster, and you'll be laughing out of the other side of your mouth." It worried her to detect anxiety hidden under his bantering cheer. Why couldn't the man ever be open and straightforward with her? She gave his chest a couple of irritated pokes with one slim finger, then walked past him into the pub, blasted by wild Irish jigging music, noisy laughter and conversation.

Riley met them with cries of joy, commenting slyly on the watermelon Merle was growing under the front of her exercise suit. Seating them in his private booth, he insisted upon surprising them with dinner, brought a pot of tea and cups, then left.

Shane made a ceremony of pouring tea for both of them, then sugared and stirred his. "Something sort of interesting happened yesterday," he offered offhandedly, glancing up at her and down again. "We've gone national."

"National what?"

"National press coverage."

"You mean your trial has?" She sat up straighter when the baby gave her a good solid kick to the ribs.

"That, yes." He lifted his cup and sipped, eyeing her cautiously over the rim. "And . . . us."

"Us?!" She puckered her brows. "As in you and me?"

"That's the us. We seem to have been mentioned in newspapers all around the country. We even made *The New York Times*." His anxiety wasn't hidden by a grin any longer as he peered at her face, testing her expression.

Her eyes went wide, her fair complexion turned pink with a horrified flush. "*The New York Times*?!"

Shane put his cup down and pursed his lips, running his hand over the back of his neck. "Let me try to explain."

"I wish you would!"

"Remember how my runaways staged a sit-in on the courthouse steps while the trial was in session on Monday? And the police came to rout them, all dressed up in riot gear? The girls made quite a splash on the front page of the *Chronicle*, standing up to them. So the syndicates picked them up as good human interest, along with Linda and Hollbrook."

"So?" Merle stared at him, gripping the edge of the table with her fingers. "Where does the *us* come into it?"

"Well, the story rather naturally led into a background piece about my cause. And me. That's when you and Ellen turned up." He cleared his throat. "And once they'd done that, they sort of picked up on the bit about how you and Miss Merry were x'd out by *YS* for aspiring to be a single parent."

"Oh, my Lord!" Merle whispered, her heart dropping as she saw her privacy evaporating.

Shane's blue eyes were sincerely apologetic. "Honest to gosh, I swear I didn't have anything to do with this. I didn't even know we'd gone national until Valerie Valerto called me today, ecstatic about having her series of articles about us and the adoption reprinted in *The New York Times*."

"Well, why didn't she call and warn *me?!*"

"Scared, probably. She's no fool."

Riley interrupted to serve dinner—a bowl of tossed salad, a thick lamb stew dappled with vegetables and potatoes, soda bread on the side—then left quickly, sensing the tense atmosphere.

Shane busied himself with serving stew and salad and slicing the bread, then folded his hands in his lap. "You're pretty upset, aren't you?"

"Of course I'm upset! What do you expect? How could something like this have happened to me when I've always been so careful?" Her dismay sparked a nervous appetite; she picked up her fork and tasted the stew. It was delicious, but after several bites she put down her fork and groaned. "My father has *The New York Times* delivered wherever he lives. I expect he and mother know by now that they're going to be grandparents. Again."

"Haven't you told them yet?" Shane peered at her, a full fork poised in front of his mouth. "Were you planning to wait until the baby is old enough to fly on down and introduce herself?"

Merle sighed, regretting the alienation that made the telling so difficult. Lately she'd been yearning more and more for the closeness and support of her parents. But she felt shy and afraid of going after it after so many years. "I suppose I'd better send a cable and try to explain. But—as one of my readers put it—they're going to have a *cow*."

At nine-thirty that evening, after driving home from the Lamaze session, Shane followed Merle into the living room and threw the two pillows on the sofa. She looked him up and down as he took off his jacket. "I've been meaning to ask all evening, did you wear that shirt to prove you have a right to be in birthing class, or what?"

His pale blue T-shirt had pink lettering: Baby on Board. "Just covering all bases," he said, taking her into his arms and kissing her on the forehead. Then he laughed and backed off to pat her belly. "That sassy kid kicked me. Can't you teach him better manners?"

"She takes after you. Who can teach her anything?" Merle smiled, then looked up at him anxiously. "What did you think of the class tonight?"

"What did I think?" He scratched his cheek contemplatively, then grinned, hiding his anxiety behind teasing. "I think it was a sight to behold, all you pregnant women lying on the floor like beached whales going hee, hee, hee. Sounded like an asthmatic audience at a comedy club."

Merle forced a scowl. "We aren't going to learn a thing about relaxation if all you do is sit around making fun of everybody."

"Oh, we'll do all right—at least we have the maturity for it. I couldn't believe how damned *young* every one of those other nine couples were. Did you notice that?"

She made a face. "How could I miss, when they

kept glancing at me as if it were perverted to be pregnant at my age." She turned serious. "Apparently you had a lot of fun tonight, but can you handle coaching me?"

He looked down, avoiding her gaze and nodded after a moment. "I think so. Lamaze will probably do me as much good as you. If I get shaky, I can use the relaxation techniques and breath myself out of my fears."

"I hope so."

"I'll make it so." He hung a crystal pendant over a lamp shade for her to focus on, making it spin slowly on its chain, flashing fragments of rainbow around the room. Then he threw the two pillows on the braided rug. "Okay, down on the floor. I'm supposed to see that you practice your exercises and breathing. I'm the boss, remember."

"Where did you come up with 'boss'?" Merle took his hands and levered herself awkwardly onto her knees, then down on her butt. "As I recollect, your title is coach."

"It boils down to the same thing, doesn't it? I get to give the orders." He helped her lie back, tucking a pillow under her head and another under her legs. Then he got down beside her on his knees. "Hide a tense muscle and stare at the pendant."

"Anything you say, coach. Okay, I'm staring, and it's hidden, find it."

Shane ran kneading hands up and down one side of her body then the other. He gave an impish grin, gently massaging her breasts. "This training should come in handy after the baby is born and things go back to normal again. Hey, watch out, no giggling. Let's hear the hee, hee, hee."

After searching her body, he sat back on his heels. "How am I supposed to find the one you hid? You must have a couple hundred tensed muscles. Is something worrying you?"

"Now what could possibly be worrying me? My life

is so simple." She gave a wry laugh and frowned at the crystal.

Shane eventually found the tensed muscle in her shoulder and massaged it soft. Then he lifted her hand and shook it gently, testing for relaxation. "Let go, darlin', you're still all tied up in knots. I'm doing my part, but you've got to cooperate. Come on, let's get it out into the open—what's bothering you. Is it the national coverage?"

She made a face. "No, it's pointless to worry about that when I've already lost everything I ever held dear."

"Then what is it?" He brought his brows down over blue eyes. "If you can't trust me with your worries, then what's the point of the relationship?"

"Well, aren't you a fine one to talk about trust and openness? You've been laughing and joking about Lamaze and labor all evening, when I know you're just as scared as—" She nipped the sentence off short.

Shane moved so that he was sitting with his hip pressed against hers and his arm braced on the floor on the other side of her body. "Okay, out with it. Scared as who, darlin'?"

"As me. I'm a coward, Shane. The closer it gets, the more scared I feel about going through labor." She pinched a nip of his T-shirt with the fingers of each hand, trying and failing at a smile. "Lately I'm not really, really sure I want to have this baby," she said, struggling to hide the real terror she felt. "I think maybe I want to back out."

He cupped his palm around her cheek, rubbing the ball of his thumb gently over his lips. "Labor can't be as bad as you think. If it were, women wouldn't still be having babies."

"How would you know? You're not one of them," she exclaimed, her fear transforming into resentment. "But I know, because lately I've begun having flashbacks of how it was when I had Ellen. And it'll probably be even worse now that I'm so much older."

Shane looked helplessly down at her. "But you've got a good doctor, and I'll be there with you, sweetheart." He lifted her up and held her against his chest.

Merle put his arms around his neck and pressed her face into the curve of his neck. "Do you promise? You really will be with me?"

"I'll be there, darlin'." He rocked back and forth, running his hand over her hair. "It'll be all right, I promise."

Merle held him tightly for a moment, then lifted her head and began drawing away. "Oh, I know you're right. I'm just being silly."

He smiled at her. "Everything will be just fine as long as we get this Lamaze business down pat."

"Right. All I've got to do is learn to relax."

Merle lay down on her side with the pillow between her knees, trying to force her mind clear of past fear and grief, breathing, hee, hee, hee. But even when Shane put his hands up under her velour shirt and kneaded his thumbs up and down her back, her muscles continued to twitch and tighten rebelliously. What she needed was something good—no, great—to happen in her life for a change. Then maybe she could relax.

Merle threw her arms around Shane when he arrived unexpectedly one afternoon in the middle of November. "Oh, Lord, am I glad to see you, love. How'd you know I wanted to talk to you? I've been trying to call, but I couldn't get a hold of you. I've got wonderful news!" She hugged him as close as she could with a belly the size of a wine cask coming between them, and kissed him exuberantly, scarcely aware that his dripping yellow poncho was drenching her. The winter rains had begun again.

"Hey, it's worth a cycle ride in the rain for a

welcome like this, darlin'." Laughing, he gathered her into his arms and kissed her. "You couldn't get me because I've been tied up tight in conferences. And I'm here because I've got big news too! But I'm getting you all wet."

He backed away and pulled the poncho off over his head, shook it out the open door, and hung it on the hat rack, then took off his jacket and hung it in the closet. His T-shirt had red letters that spelled: I Survived The Big One of '89. Knowing full well he was driving her wild with impatience, he glanced at her, blue eyes dancing. "What's your news? Did Dr. Shapiro decide we're having twins after all?"

"Not hardly. He says I'm not big enough, even though I feel like a hippopotamus." She decided to serve him impatience, tit for tat, and rested her folded arms on the shelf jutting out under the front of her yellow bib overalls. "My news will wait, you rode through the rain and earned the right to go first. What's yours?"

His grin added sunshine to the dreary storm light coming through the windows of the entry. "Hollbrook has agreed to settle out of court."

She stared at him for a moment, then grabbed his hands, her smile rivaling his. "You mean it's over—*finally*. But why is he? You kept telling me they had the upper hand."

Shane lifted her hands and kissed each one. "It was the national publicity. He couldn't stand having the entire country see his name dragged through the mud, so he wants out." He gave a laugh. "I guess he's as concerned about his reputation as you are. Thank goodness."

She laughed too, delighted for him. "What kind of a settlement?"

"We'll be negotiating for some time, but Linda stands to end up with an extremely generous award, not that money can make up for her lost past. And . . ." He couldn't stop grinning. "*And*, Hollbrook is setting up a trust fund to be used to establish the first anonymous safe house for my runaways. It's a beginning."

She threw her arms around his neck and kissed him all over his face. "I am absolutely thrilled for you, darling."

"Yeah," he agreed, sighing. "So that's my news, now what's yours?"

Merle laughed happily. "To tell it right, I have to show you."

Linking her arm through his, she led him to the sun-room, beyond the kitchen. Misty rain had dappled the half circle of windows with diamond droplets, backed by gray clouds. Two large cardboard cartons were sitting on the table. Dipping her hands into one carton, she lifted a bundle of envelopes and let them flutter back down.

She couldn't stop smiling, her heart was that full. "Louise brought these letters to me yesterday. They're from irate teen girls and their parents protesting Miss Merry's retirement. I guess they started coming as soon as my column was withdrawn from *Youngest Sister*. But when the reason for my retirement went national, the mail quadrupled. My teenyboppers are threatening to boycott *YS*, Shane! And all because of you and your publicity." She plunged her hands into the box again and lifted two handfuls.

He stared at the letters streaming down from her fingers. "Good grief! How does it feel to know half the population of the United States loves you?"

"It's humbling."

"I should think so. What happens now?"

She put her hand on his arm and laughed in pure malicious joy. "Louise warned me that the bigwigs were sweating, and to be prepared for a call. And she was right, Simmons called this morning. She almost begged Miss Merry to come back. Oh, Shane, I've been walking three feet off the ground ever since. And that says something, bulky as I am."

"That's fantastic, darlin'!" Shane grabbed her into his arms and kissed her soundly.

"Fantastic? It's incredible!" she exclaimed, kissing him back. "What amazes me is that I've been fighting your publicity all this time. And here that's the very thing that solved my problem. Both our problems. I'm ready to eat crow—you were right and I was wrong. My reputation didn't mean diddly squat to anyone. All my worrying was wasted effort."

"Yeah." He grinned down at her. "Funny, isn't it? A week ago I was swamped and you were out of a job, and now I'm going on the unemployed roster and you're jumping back in."

She clapped her hands enthusiastically on his cheeks. "Unemployed, my left foot! I've never known a lawyer to come out of a case poorer. I bet you plan to take your share out of Hollbrook, don't you?"

Making a modest face, he admitted, "Oh, I imagine I'll get mine."

She laughed. "Well, so am I going to get my share too. Bless Louise for warning me and pointing out the situation. I was all ready for Simmons with a list of demands when she called. First and foremost I'm insisting upon total autonomy over the content of my column. And the freedom to work at home with a computer link to *YS* as much as I want. And I'm sure I can talk them into at least doubling my salary. Then I can afford a nanny to help take care of little Oops." She sighed happily. "Oh, Lord, it feels good to have everything under control, right under my thumb again."

Shane stared down into her face, his grin fading. "A *nanny*? Why?"

Merle backed out of the embrace and looked up at him questioningly. "I should think that's obvious—to take care of the baby at home when I have to leave and while I work. So he/she can have stability, remember—no shuffling."

"I see." He pulled a chair out from the table and sat

down, propping one ankle on the other knee and scowling as he picked at the frayed hem of his jeans.

Merle leaned one hand on the edge of the table and braced the other fist on her hip, first mystified, then resentful over his attitude. "Will you please tell me what you're upset about? If you don't mind."

"In case you didn't tumble to it," he said, matching her icy politeness, "part of my news is that I'll be free to help you with the baby now that my case is over. Then all of a sudden I find out I'm being replaced by a nanny, and you've got your life all planned and organized without me. I don't have to be hit over the head with a sledgehammer to know when I've been cut, dried, and shut out."

She narrowed her brown eyes and folded both arms over the mound under her bib overalls. "How can you possibly see hiring a nanny as shutting you out?"

"Well, I certainly don't see it as committing yourself to me," he answered.

"Well, you certainly aren't demonstrating any reason why I should commit, with that attitude. I thought you'd be happy about Miss Merry's resurrection, and that for once I'm smart enough not to sell myself short."

Glancing at the rain-washed window, Shane rubbed his chest over the word "Survived" on his T-shirt, then looked at Merle. "I *am* glad you're going to be Miss Merry again. It's just that I got used to things the way they've been for the last couple of months. Maybe it's chauvinistic, but I kind of liked you being a little dependent on me. It made me feel important and special." He worked at dredging up a smile, a stilted curving of the lips. "I know, I know—you're going to remind me about equal rights."

Merle stared at him, hurt and angry, and not even sure why. Fighting might have been preferable to this too polite, too civilized discussion that wasn't resolving a thing. It occurred to her that the issue wasn't her working, or nannys, or even commitment. She couldn't fathom what *was* holding mutual trust at bay. *What?*

The blank look on Shane's face made her want to reach out and shake him, scream at him, force him to talk to her! How ridiculous, when she wasn't any more open than he. She loved him so much, so deeply, and he loved her too. But every emotional word they didn't say added another brick to the wall shoving them farther and farther apart.

A panicky premonition came over her. It terrified her to feel too many emotions pushing up toward the surface of her subconscious, getting ready to explode. They were too powerful. She was terrified they would destroy everything, but she didn't know how to defuse them.

Twelve

Dear Miss Merry,
I'm so happy your column will be back in next month's Youngest Sister. *No one understands us kids like you. I want you to know I've decided to keep my baby. My folks are being real good about it, so I'm trying to hide how scared, upset, and even mad I feel. I need to ask, did you ever feel really happy again after you went through this?*

Cindy Jones

Dear Cindy,
Love, it's perfectly normal to feel anger, fear, and depression in your situation. Hiding or burying these feelings gives them more power than they warrant. So talk them out with someone you trust, darling, and then you will still have a wonderful, happy life in store for you.

Miss Merry

At six-thirty P.M. on the last Friday in November, Merle stood at the window watching Shane slither and splash up the driveway on his motorcycle. She felt edgy, irritable, and weepy. As much as anything her mood had to do with the unrelenting rain that had been falling for days and days from a low pressure system stuck over the Bay Area. She peered at the hillside below her house. Both the plastic and topsoil had wrinkled up in several areas, leaving earth-colored slashes.

Shane's mood was as testy as hers, judging by the expression on his face when he came in. This night was the final session of Lamaze: The movie of a live birth. Merle suspected he was dreading the session though they hadn't discussed it. "You sure you want to go out in this kind of weather?" he grumbled, yanking his yellow poncho over his head, showering droplets on the entry tiles.

"I won't be out in the weather, I'll be in a car. Unless you have some absurd idea that I'm going to ride on your motorcycle."

The instant the words were out, she regretted her flip answer. She couldn't seem to rise above the defensive distance their relationship had fallen into. It was far more useless than their bickering had been, and made her feel frustrated and angry—at herself as well as at Shane. Her mind echoed the question printed in big black letters on the gray T-shirt under his leather jacket: Why?

"You mean you really are going to trust me to hot-rod your car down the freeway?" Shane said, matching her glib evasiveness. Apparently his despair matched hers, too, because he held her tightly in his arms for several moments, as if she might try to push him away or disappear. There wasn't any life in his smile when he backed off and patted her monumental front. "What's with the kid? He restless or something?"

She blew out a tired breath. "All day—both of us have been. If he feels half as miserable as I do, it's no wonder he's kicking."

"Why? What's wrong?" he asked apprehensively.

"Oh, nothing, really. I had this odd impulse to sort through my belongings and clean house today. Now I feel weary and backachy on top of being grouchy. And look at my dress. I'm such a blimp, I barely fit into a sack." She slapped at the stretched gathers of her smocked brown jumper. "What's wrong is that I'm sick up to here of being pregnant. There now, aren't you sorry you asked?"

"Hang in there, darlin'," he said, putting his arm around her shoulders. "There's only a month left."

"But that's half the problem—the closer it comes, the scareder I get. Now I have to watch this stupid birth movie tonight and be reminded of what I have to look forward to."

His face brightened. "Then let's not go. We've had all the relaxation and hee-hee-hee training. That's all we really need, isn't it?"

"It's part of the course, so it must be useful. We might as well just go and get it over with."

He shoved his hands into his pockets and changed the subject. "Did you know there's a new slide beside your driveway?"

"No, I didn't." Merle went back to the living room to look out the window. It was too dark to see now.

Shane followed to stand beside her. "When the storm passes, we'll have someone put in terraces to hold the earth in place. But for now I think you'd better move into the houseboat with me. A couple more days of heavy rain could put your house in the middle of the freeway."

Merle stared at the strings of stationary headlights jamming the six eastbound lanes down below, and trails of flashing red taillights going westward. Her heart sank at the thought of losing her beautiful house. Especially the baby's room, the nest she and Shane had built—probably the only amicable thing they'd done since coming back together—outside of making love, that is.

"I can guess how you feel," he said softly. "The house has grown on me too. I kind of like sitting up here so high, watching the seasons change over the valley."

She nodded mournfully. "There isn't anything we can do right now, so we'd better go finish out our Lamaze course. But I have to go to the bathroom first. I swear that's all I've been doing all day. Every twenty minutes."

When she came back, Shane was still standing in front of the living room window, hands in his jeans pockets, jingling change. "Well, come on," she exclaimed. "I don't want to be late."

"Merry, let's pass on the movie, okay?" He looked back, his shoulders held straight, his spine stiff under his jacket.

The timbre of his voice sent anxiety surging through her system. She walked into the living room and levered herself awkwardly down to huddle in the corner of the ruffled sofa. "You've been trying to wiggle out of this last Lamaze session all week, haven't you? What's going on, Shane?"

He took a deep breath and let it out, tried to grin but couldn't. "The thought of watching some woman give birth gives me the shakes. I'll be damned if I'm going down there to keel over in front of all those kid parents."

"But if you can't cope with a movie, how can you handle the real thing?"

"That's different! That'll be you."

"No, it isn't that much different." Merle's thickly fringed brown eyes grew enormous as her confidence deteriorated. "You aren't going to be with me when I have the baby, are you, Shane?"

He took off his leather jacket and threw it on a chair. The back of his T-shirt said, Why Not? to counter the "Why" on the front. Dropping down beside her on the sofa, his tall, muscular body slouched, he insisted, "I'll be with you, Merry. I promise."

"You promise? But how can I trust your promises?" A dam somewhere inside seemed to break. A geyser of leftover sixteen-year-old terrors erupted from her subconscious, sweeping away all adult logic. She didn't even recognize her shrill voice when she cried, "What am I going to do? Who's going to be with me when I have the baby? I don't want to do it alone. I can't! Not again!"

Shane reached out and took her face between his two hands, trying to ground her. "Merry, I will be with you, but I just don't see the point in watching a movie about having a baby. I've talked to all the mothers in my family, and they've told me what it's like. I know everything I need to know."

"They told—? How can you possibly know what having a baby is like by listening to someone describe it?" She hitched forward, floundering when she tried to get up off the sofa. "Oh, I hate this! I have to go to the bathroom, and I can't even get up!"

"Here, I'll give you a hand." He jumped up and boosted her to her feet.

When Merle came back, she planted herself in front of Shane, taking up where she'd left off, but in control again. "Isn't that just like a man? To think you know everything because you talked to people. Well, you have no concept of what labor is like! But I do! I remember exactly how it was when I had Ellen."

A mix of anger and terror stamped through her. She grabbed the front of his T-shirt with her fists. He winced and grabbed her wrists. "And you weren't there either, damn you!" she cried out. "*I needed you!*" When she realized her precious control had slipped, she put her hands over her face and started to turn away.

Shane grabbed her arms. "Will you quit hiding from me! You're always doing that, touching on something important, then snatching it back. I'm sick and tired of being shut out."

Merle tried ineffectively to jerk away from his hands, anger contorting her delicate face. "*You* being shut out?! You, the one who bickers about little things and jokes away the big stuff? The one who pulls shutters over your feelings if I get too close?"

Heat lightning flickered in his light blue eyes, but he pressed his lips together for several seconds and managed to fight his demons down. "Okay. Okay, there must be an ocean of things that both of us need to say. So let's start at the beginning. Will you please, once and for all, tell me what happened when we were kids, after I went into the army."

Merle jutted her dimpled chin out. "You're right, things do need to be said. But I don't want to . . . I can't possibly make you understand how it felt to—" She broke off and swallowed convulsively, feeling naked, terrified of surrendering to vulnerability.

"Damm it, Merry, don't stop now, say it. To . . . what?"

Tears glimmered in her huge brown eyes as she looked up at him. "To . . . to love you . . . so much. You were my life, my entire existence, Shane. But then you went into the army and just drifted away and forgot me."

"You really felt that way, Merry?" he asked in a husky whisper. "Go on, tell me the rest."

She shook her head, afraid, feeling as if a pit full of vipers was opening up in front of her. "I can't."

He pressed her hands against his chest when she tried to pull free. "Don't push me away. Tell me what you felt!"

"All right!" she cried out. "You were my life, but you left me and went flitting off, having fun and looking so handsome in that damned uniform of yours. While I had to carry your baby in me for nine months. I was in labor thirty-six hours, terrified and fighting it all the way, no one to help me go hee, hee, hee. I begged and screamed for you, but *you weren't there!* She pinched her eyes shut and gave a low cry in her throat.

He touched the silver-gold waves of hair at the side of her face. "Aw, Merry, I'm so sorry . . . so sorry."

She opened her eyes and looked up into his face, but saw only the past. "When the baby came they laid that tiny little bit of you and me on my stomach. I put my two hands around her head and she looked at me. Then they took her away, and it was as if both you and the baby were dead."

The pain of it surged up from where she'd buried it. But Merle, who went teary-eyed over every emotional twitch, couldn't cry over the tragedy. "I grieved over her and over you for months, maybe years, maybe I never quit. I didn't have anyone to talk to, so finally I just buried my feelings so I could get on with my life."

Shane reached out to take her into his arms. "I wish I'd known."

"Why didn't you know? You should have!" she cried furiously, pushing him away. "Let me go, I've got to go to the damned bathroom again."

When Merle came back to the living room, she stood far away from him at the window. Anger flushed her face and set off sparks in her dark eyes. "Damn you, Shane Halloran! It . . . everything . . . was so good with you. You ruined me for any other man! You robbed me of any happiness I might have had in life. How dare you pop back into my life and expect me to act as if nothing had ever happened!"

He stared at her for a moment, then limped across the room and squared himself off in front of her, booted feet spread, hands hanging by his sides in fists. "What makes you think you've got a corner on pain and grief? I damn well was not flitting around having fun and games in a uniform like you seem to think! Look at me, can you picture me as a soldier? I should have burned my damned draft card and run to Canada. But I had a mistaken impression that we were going to get married, so I went into the army instead. And then—"

His face twisted with his struggle to bring a forbidden subject out into the open. Then he seemed to lose and began to turn away. Merle stepped quickly forward and grabbed his arm. "Oh no you don't! You made me tell you what happened on my side back then. Now you have to tell me your side. I need to know!"

His bicep went rigid under her hand. He wouldn't look into her face, staring instead at the baby straining out against her brown jumper. "I was so homesick in boot camp," he said in a low, terse voice. "I lived for your letters. When you quit writing, I was so naive and trusting that I imagined you must have gotten sick or maybe died."

"I didn't quit writing!"

"Well, I quit getting letters!" Shane roared. Jerking away from her hand, he turned and hit the window frame with his fist. "And when I came home on leave your parents told me your crush on me had fizzled out."

"My *crush!*" she whispered with numb disbelief. "Why would they tell you something like that?"

"How should I know?! But, oh, Lord, it hurt. After all we'd shared and all I felt for you—to find out I'd only been a crush!"

"You did care?" She clasped her hands in front of the smocking on her brown jumper, gazing yearningly at his broad back, turned implacably toward her.

"Of course I cared! How could you have ever thought anything different?" He pressed his forehead to the window pane. "The army sent me overseas to Nam right after that. Cripes, you know me—I'm no killer. But there I was out in the jungle heartsick over you and scared out of my skull, surrounded by a bunch of strangers they said were my enemies. I never fired a shot, but I got hit in the first battle I was in."

He bent his head back and took a deep breath before he could go on. "I lay in the jungle with my leg rotting for six hours before they got me out. Delirious half the time. I kept thinking I saw you picking your way through the brush, coming to me. And then I cried every time I realized you weren't there.

"I spent three months in a military hospital and lost count of the surgeries. They gave me shots for every damned thing under the sun, but there wasn't any shot to cure me of you. And I was hurting twice as bad over you than any physical pain." He snorted a humorless laugh. "I came to the conclusion you'd dumped me because I wasn't good enough."

"Shane, no, I never thought that." She pressed her clasped hands against her mouth. "Never!"

"How could I know that when you'd disappeared?" he demanded. "I went into law school when I got home, I suppose because I felt I had to prove something to you, even though we were through." Turning to face her, he leaned his shoulder on the window frame and twisted his mouth into a bitter smile. "It was fairly disillusioning to find out I was the same man, even after I had the degree. That's why I decided to steer clear of you when I found out you'd come back to the Bay Area."

He stared at her with smoldering, angry blue eyes for a few moments. "I've felt a hell of a lot of rage and hate at you, too, in my day, kiddo. I probably never got over it, or you. You say I ruined your life. Well, you didn't exactly lay the groundwork for peace and contentment in mine either."

The agony Merle felt might have been because her heart was breaking all over again, or it might have been caused by his bitter words cutting through her like a sword—she couldn't tell. All she knew for certain was that she loved him so much, more than she ever had as a silly kid, and this moment felt like

the end of everything. She started to reach out
hand but let it drop. The distance between them ha
grown so great, she couldn't reach him, though onl
two steps separated them.

She plodded to the bathroom once again, numbe
by the unfairness of it all, the uselessness of the pai
their separation had caused. When she came back
she shook her head sadly. "I wish I could. I want to s
badly, but I just can't seem to forget or forgive, o
trust again."

Her loneliness was reflected in Shane's face. "
know, Merry. Believe me, I know," he said in a thick
husky voice. "I love you so much, but there's all tha
trash holding us apart." Suddenly he made a tor
mented sound in his throat and covered his face wit
his hands, his shoulders heaving.

Merle stared at him. The muffled sound of hi
weeping cracked the dam she'd built around he
emotions so many years ago. The tears in her sou
swelled up against the crack until it seemed sh
would burst. Wrapping her arms around her ponder
ous body, she threw back her head and keened for a
the pain and grief they'd both suffered. For th
hopelessness she felt now. When the storm finall
passed, there was a great emptiness inside her. A
fearful vacuum.

Shane took a deep, shuddering breath, then pulle
out the tail of his T-shirt and wiped his face. His fac
looked as empty as she felt when he held out hi
hand. "Do you think there's any hope at all for us
Merry?" he whispered.

She put her hand in his, clutching his finger
desperately. They stood connected but so far apart
"Oh, Shane, how can there be when we can't lay ou
past to rest?"

Thirteen

My darling Merle,

Since your cable arrived, your father and I have talked endlessly about you, regretting the mistakes we made in the past. You grew up in a world where the old familiar rules and morals were turning upside down, and we mistakenly thought we were protecting you when we withheld Shane Halloran's letters from you and advised your aunt and uncle to waylay your letters to him. All we accomplished was to drive our only daughter away from us.

Now that you have become a mother, we pray you can find it in your heart to forgive us. We ache to rebuild a loving relationship with you, and to know your unique and talented Shane. Our amazement and joy over having not only two grandchildren, but a great-grandchild *on the way is more than . . .*

The letter! Merle had forgotten it in the heat of battle. If she'd told Shane about it as soon as he'd come, instead of saving it for later, maybe they could have talked their feelings out rationally. Now it was too late; they'd already said horrible things to each other. Clinging to his hand, loving him so terribly, she felt panicked by a sense of emptiness. She felt like a husk with nothing inside.

That's why it was such a shock to feel a copious amount of hot liquid gushing down her legs. A mix of embarrassment, horror, and surprise dashed the despair and yearning out of her mind. She stared down at a wet circle spreading on the braided rug under her feet. "Shane . . . ? Either I just wet my pants or my water broke."

Her announcement shocked his own personal despair off his face. "Say *what?*"

"You don't suppose I've been going to the bathroom so often because I'm in labor, do you?"

It took about five seconds for that to sink in and for the color to fade out of his face. "Merry, of course you can't be in labor!" he said quite logically. "We haven't decided on a name for the baby yet."

She stood rooted to the spot, staring at him with astonished dark eyes.

"What's the matter?" he asked, peering back.

"I'm having a contraction." She felt more disbelief and curiosity than discomfort.

He bounded forward and grabbed her upper arms. "Oh, cripes, Merry! Is it bad?"

She gave a laugh. "Shane, you aren't supposed to ask if it's bad, you're supposed to tell me to breathe."

"Breathe, then—hee, hee." He looked around frantically. "Where's the stupid crystal you're supposed to focus on?"

"I don't know. I put it somewhere when I was sorting through things today. Never mind, the contraction is over." Then reality struck, anxiety on its heels. "Shane, if I'm in labor, that means our baby will be premature! What if she's too small and weak? What if we lose her after all?"

When she panicked, he pulled himself together and

put his arms around her. "Nothing will go wrong with the baby, darlin'," he said, his voice as solid and supportive as his arms. "Eight months isn't that early."

Putting her hands flat on his chest, she looked pleadingly up at him. "I can't remember what we're supposed to do now."

He brushed back her hair with one big hand. "Don't worry, Merry darlin', there's plenty of time. You go get cleaned up, and I'll call the doctor."

It occurred to her that Shane was working hard to keep his voice calm, and that anchored her. She struggled to compose herself for his sake, if no other. "Yes, I'll get cleaned up, and you call Dr. Shapiro."

Spurred by increasing urgency, Merle managed to shower, put on a pink knit smock, maternity jeans, and running shoes in record time. Then she hurried as best she could back to the living room. "Shane, I had another contraction. What did the doctor say?"

Shane was standing in the middle of the room, shifting from one foot to the other. "I didn't talk to him. The phone's dead. This stupid storm must have knocked it out."

Her heart leaped. "Dead? The phone! But what are we going to do? Good Lord, I'm having another one. It isn't even ten minutes!" This contraction was strong enough to remind her to breathe.

Shane stepped behind her and rubbed the curve where her neck met her shoulders with his thumbs, talking her through. When it was over, he raked his fingers through his silver-black hair, standing the curl on end. "Maybe I should drive you directly to the hospital in your car, without talking to Dr. Shapiro first."

"Yes, good idea, that's what we'll do." Merle turned and headed toward the door to the garage.

Shane grabbed his jacket and followed on her heels, then stopped short. "Wait, it's still pouring pitchforks. You need a coat, Merry!" He snatched her raincoat out of the closet, jammed her arms through the sleeves, and tied the belt over the gap where it didn't meet in front. Then he hustled her out the door.

Rain drummed on the roof of the garage and the air smelled musty as he boosted her into the passenger seat and fastened the seat belt around her. Struggling into his black leather jacket on the run, he circled the car and jumped into the driver's seat. "Okay, no problem. Gimme the key!"

She stared wide-eyed at him. "I don't have it."

"Well, where is it?" He sounded as if he were verging on hysteria.

"Let me think . . . maybe it's in my purse on the shelf in the coat closet. But hurry, I'm having another."

At an all-out gallop it took Shane less than thirty seconds to come back and hop in the car with the key ring. The garage door went up automatically. The engine started with the first try, but he killed it backing the car out. Grinding his teeth, he started it again, backed out, and came around to aim down the hill. The headlights dug twin tunnels into the dark night as he drove in second gear down the driveway. Rain poured out of the sky in great sheets, throwing up spray as it hit the asphalt.

"Oh, damn!" Shane jammed his boot on the brake, the car skidding to the very brink of the gaping trench that had appeared in the headlights. The driveway was gone.

Merle stared through the windshield, watching another chunk of asphalt break away and fall into the deep washout. She turned her head and peered at Shane. "What are we going to do now?"

His face looked greenish in the fluorescent light of the instrument panel. "What are we going to do . . . ? What *are* we going to do? We aren't going to panic, that's what we aren't going to do." He hit the steering wheel with the palms of his hands. "Well, what's wrong with me? I can get the cycle down around the slide and go for help."

Reversing the car, spinning the wheels and burning rubber, he backed up the driveway and into the garage again. Running around the car, he boosted Merle out. "You stay in the house while I go to the police station. Probably they can bring in a helicopter to take you out."

She grabbed his arm as he was turning toward the cycle. "You're out of your mind if you think I'm going to stay here alone."

Another contraction began. This time she breathed, hee, hee, hee. It was a long one and she was glad to have Shane keeping her on track. When it was over she said, "No, sir! If you go, I'm going with you."

He stared at her, his eyes pleading. "Merry, for God's sake, be reasonable. We're talking about a motorcycle, remember? It's too dangerous for a woman in your condition." When he saw he wasn't making any impression, he lifted his hands in desperation. "But you've always been afraid to ride the cycle—remember?"

Rain pattered on the garage roof as she peered at him through the night shadows. "I guess I'm not afraid any longer," she said, surprised to realize it was true. "I'll feel safer with you, even on the cycle, than anywhere else or with anyone else."

He looked questioningly at her for a moment. "You wouldn't be saying you trust me, would you?"

"I think I must be."

"Why, Merry? Why now of all times, after all the hurtful things I've said to you?"

Cupping his cheeks with her hands, she searched his face and saw no shutters, no joking. "Oh, I wish I'd told you about the letter from my parents before we fought. They broke us up by keeping your letters from me and mine from you. I've never had a reason to mistrust your love."

"So that's what happened." He turned his head and kissed her fingertips. "Trust is a rare, beautiful thing."

Shane talked her through another contraction then. "That was a long one," he said anxiously when it was over. "Maybe you're right, we'd better give the cycle a try." He glanced at the mound jutting out between the sides of her coat and ran back into the house to get his voluminous poncho. "Here, put this on to keep little Oops dry."

After he'd threaded the neckhole over her head and tied the hood around her face, she looked down at herself. "Good grief, I look like something four people could sleep in on a camping trip."

"For cripes' sake, this isn't the time or the place for vanity!" he said with a hollow laugh, his sense of humor failing him. He rushed across the garage to wheel the motorcycle out.

Even with the yard light on, the hillside was very dark and almost as slippery as a water slide. Merle stood out of the rain in the open garage door and hee, hee, hee'd through two contractions while Shane alternately dragged and scooted the bulky cycle down the hill and around the slide by brute force. After parking it on the driveway below the washout, he climbed back up to her side.

"Okay, hold on to my neck," he said, taking a firm grip on Merle around her back with one arm. Then, propping her against his side, he slipped and skidded down the hill, using his other arm as a brace. When their feet slid out from under them, he twisted to cushion her fall with his body.

"Are you okay, darlin'?" he asked, heaving up on an elbow, his hair plastered to his skull, water dribbling down his muddy face.

"I think so." She struggled up to a sitting position, the poncho spread out in a curtain around her, and shook mud off her hands. Then she threw her face back to the storm and burst into laughter.

"This is no joke, Merry!" Shane bellowed, struggling for a foothold on the slick hillside. "What's so damn funny?"

"Us!" she exclaimed. "Would anyone else in the world be caught in a situation like this, at a time like this?"

A contraction struck just then, and she breathed between whoops of laughter.

By the time it was over, Shane was laughing too. "We do seem to be a matched pair, don't we?" He dragged her up onto her feet, maneuvered her around the cave-in, and finally onto the driveway, where the motorcycle was parked. He held her in his arms, breathing hard. "Don't be afraid, I'll get you out of this pickle yet, you wait and see."

"I know it, and I'm not afraid, love," she said. "But I think we'd better hurry."

"Cripes, don't tell me that. Trusting me stretches only so far, remember." He jammed the helmet down over the poncho hood on her head, fastened the strap with fumbling fingers, then boosted her onto the pallet behind his saddle. Mounting, he pulled her arms around his waist. "Hang on, damm it! If you fall off and go bouncing down the road, I'll never forgive myself."

Bowed over the baby between them, Merle clung to him with both arms. For a time she felt a disorienting sense of unbalance as the motorcycle moved down the driveway, led through the dark by the single tunnel of light. But that passed by the time they reached the access road.

At the diamond freeway interchange Shane stopped and lifted her visor so she could hear. "Where's the police station? I figure they should have someone there who knows about having babies."

Merle narrowed her eyes and set her dimpled chin. "I absolutely refuse to have some kid cop deliver my baby! It's only a half-hour trip at most to the hospital. Let's go."

"Don't be an idiot! You can't ride all that way on this cycle. You need an ambulance!"

"Will you—hee, hee—quit wasting time by bickering," she shouted over the engine roar. "I feel like pushing."

"Oh, cripes!" Shane slammed the visor down over her face and hunched himself over the handlebars.

By the time they reached the hospital, Merle was puffing in tiny panting breaths. He swayed around the turn and entered the curved drive. When he roared up to the ambulance entrance, the double glass doors swished open automatically in front of him.

Without a moment's hesitation he gunned the motor and slewed the cycle directly into the emergency room, cutting the engine in front of the goggle-eyed nurses and resident doctor behind the desk. Jamming the kickstand down, he slung one long leg over the handlebars and dismounted, rain streaming off his hair and down his face. His leather jacket was wet and slick, his boots and jeans soaked and muddy.

Tenderly he lifted Merle off the pallet, black helmet, yellow poncho, mud-caked running shoes and all, and held her in his arms. Everyone at the desk was still rooted to their spots. "Can't you see Miss Merry is having a baby? Where the hell do you want her?" he bellowed.

Three hours later Merle was lying in bed with her head elevated, clean and dry in a blue hospital gown, feeling blessedly flat in the middle. The storm had passed, and the clouds were breaking up. Through the window the morning star could be seen glittering in the pinkening eastern sky. But she didn't notice any of that as she gazed with awe and boundless love at the miracle, the baby boy in her arms.

He'd weighed in at only five pounds two ounces,

but everyone assured her he was strong and healthy. His head was covered with fuzzy black hair, which sprouted out in every direction and was sure to be curly, and he had a deep dimple in his tiny chin. He was staring back at her with intent curiosity, but she couldn't tell if his eyes were blue or brown. "His face looks like crumpled pink rose petals, doesn't it?" she whispered, glancing at Shane.

"He's something, all right." Wearing the surgery greens they'd given him for the delivery, he was sitting on the bed.

She smiled at the tender expression on his face. "Do you want to hold him?"

"I thought you'd never ask. Come to papa." He took the blanket-cocooned mite into his big hands and nuzzled his lips against the soft head. Then he matched the baby's serious frown. "What would you like us to name you, fella?" He raised his brows at Merle. "What do you think, Mummy?"

"I'm not sure. But it has to be a very special name, because he's bound to be an individual in his own right, considering the rambunctious way he came into the world." She smiled. "I have a feeling your son is going to give even you a run for your money, love."

"That could be." He grinned down at the baby. "You're no respecter of convention and organization, are you, little one?" He looked up at Merle. "Would you have an appropriate name in mind?"

"Yes, I think so. Your parents Americanized your name, so it seems only fitting that we put the Irish back in this Halloran and name him Sean. What do you think?"

His lips twitched into a touched smile. "You're sure you care to risk two of us?"

Merle laughed, her dark eyes sparkling. "If I haven't learned anything else since you came back into my life, Shane Halloran, I've learned there are certain benefits to taking risks."

His grin spread across his face, lopsided on the

right. "Sean it is, then. But don't say I didn't warn you."

After a nurse had carried the baby away, Shane took Merle's hand and kissed her palm. "You must be exhausted, darlin'. Do you want me to leave so you can sleep?"

"No, stay—we need to talk." She turned her hand over to clasp his tightly, worried suddenly. "Shane, I wish I hadn't said those horrible things to you last night. I don't hate you, I never did. I was just so hurt."

He nodded and took her other hand too. "I know, darlin', I understand. It was the same for me. But don't wish you hadn't said it. We both vented feelings that should have been aired long ago, before they ripened and got pithy with age."

She frowned slightly, thinking about the things they'd said. "Did you really love me as much as you said you did, back when we were kids?"

"Love you! You were my life, Merry, my everything. I loved you so much it was as if I were nothing after we parted. I couldn't even pretend to love anyone else, darlin'. That's why my marriage didn't work, I suppose. It wasn't that I couldn't love, but that I couldn't love anyone but you."

"How odd," she said wonderingly. "And all those years I thought I'd been rejected."

"Never that." He pressed her two hands against his chest and asked softly, "And you, did you really love me as much as you said too?"

"I did, oh yes, my sweet, my Shane," she whispered, almost overpowered by the strength of her love, now that she was free to feel it. "You were my soul and my spirit. And I couldn't love anyone but you either. I still love you that much, I've never quit. I *couldn't* quit, even when I wanted to."

"Me either—you're still my life, Merry. That'll never change, no matter what happens between us." He lifted her hands and kissed first one, then the other.

"Now that we've finally been honest and open with each other, maybe we'll be able to tear down the wall between us."

Merle studied his face for a moment. The shutters were gone and his eyes radiated a yearning, fearful desire to hope, along with open love and need for her. His love flowed into her, filling the inner emptiness left by releasing the anger and grief. "I think we already have," she said softly.

Leaning forward, Shane circled his arms around her shoulders. "If the wall is down, do you suppose we've finally exorcised those demons of ours too?"

She clasped her hands behind his neck. "How can we tell? We're both too overawed by everything that happened this night to get into a fight."

"Let me ask you this for a test," he said, his eyes sparkling with the answer. "Was having a baby as terrifying and painful as you expected?"

She gave a surprised laugh. "Everything went so fast, I forgot to worry about how bad it was going to be, so it wasn't. Or maybe it was because you were there beside me all the way."

He looked proud but a little sheepish. "I did manage to hang in there without conking out, didn't I? Doesn't the way we reacted in a crisis tell you something?"

"Well, yes, maybe it does." She made a face. "It also tells me the doctor and the nurses must have thought we were insane bawling like a couple of banshees after the baby was born."

"Who cares about them? We needed to get all that weeping and mourning out of our systems, *finally*."

Shifting wearily on the bed, Shane moved closer to hold her more securely in his arms. "Do you remember when I asked you what you wished that time, and you said you wished we could start over? Well, this is it, darlin'. The past is wiped out, and the future is ours to shape any way we like. Maybe, just maybe, we're ready to begin building something solid for ourselves."

They stared at each other, and it was as if they were seeing each other for the first time.

"But we still don't have much in common," she said, reluctant to give in to hope, fearful of disappointment. "I'm worried that we'll still be bickering and fussing at each other."

He kissed the tip of her nose and grinned. "There's nothing wrong with bickering if the demons are gone, now is there? It might even add spice to our life. We're a fairly even match, after all."

She couldn't help smiling when she looked into his teasing eyes. "You're always so clever at putting things into perspective, aren't you?" Sighing deeply, freely, she laid her head on his shoulder and surrendered to love, hope, and the future.

Shane gently petted her silken white-gold waves of hair, then asked after a few minutes of silence, "What are you thinking?"

"Oh, I don't know—just regretting all the years we've wasted, I guess. It seems a shame to waste another minute, doesn't it? Is that marriage proposal of yours still open?"

A tender look came over his face. "Miss Merry Pierce, my own darlin', it'll be open whenever you decide you want me. Because I'll still be wanting you until the end of time."

"Well, Shane Halloran, my sweet, my love, I think it's safe to say I'll want you at least that long too." She put one hand on either side of his unshaven face and kissed him. "And beyond that to eternity."

Lifting her up from the raised head of the bed, he cradled her against his strong chest and buried his face in her hair. "I love you, Merry, so much . . . so much."

"Oh, my sweet, I love you, too, with all my heart." She kissed his neck, then the fluff of black chest hair peeking out of the V neck of his surgical gown. "I'd say we've pretty well worked out our problems, wouldn't you?"

"It looks like it, darlin'."

She grinned mischievously. "Does that mean we can be lovers again?"

A blue crystalline sparkle gleamed in his eyes. "Why, Miss Merry, how you talk! What about your reputation?"

"My what?" She widened her eyes and puckered her lips to mime a kiss.

He didn't need any more of an invitation. Bending his head, he covered her mouth and explored teasingly with his tongue to give her a hint of things to come.

She curled her hand around his thigh and whispered against his lips, "Dr. Shapiro says I have to wait six weeks before . . ."

"I don't begrudge a few weeks, darlin', not when we've got the rest of our lives." Shane's big, lopsided grin crept over his face. "Besides, once you get home, we'll find lots of other ways . . ."

THE EDITOR'S CORNER

As summer draws to a close, the nights get colder, and what better way could there be to warm up than by reading these fabulous LOVESWEPTs we have in store for you next month.

Joan Elliott Pickart leads the list with THE DEVIL IN STONE, LOVESWEPT #492, a powerful story of a love that flourishes despite difficult circumstances. When Robert Stone charges into Winter Holt's craft shop, he's a warrior on the warpath, out to expose a con artist. But he quickly realizes Winter is as honest as the day is long, and as beautiful as the desert sunrise. He longs to kiss away the sadness in her eyes, but she's vowed never to give her heart to another man—especially one who runs his life by a schedule and believes that love can be planned. It takes a lot of thrilling persuasion before Robert can convince Winter that their very different lives can be bridged. This is a romance to be cherished.

Humorous and emotional, playful and poignant, HEART OF DIXIE, LOVESWEPT #493, is another winner from Tami Hoag. Who can resist Jake Gannon, with his well-muscled body and blue eyes a girl can drown in? Dixie La Fontaine sure tries as she tows his overheated car to Mare's Nest, South Carolina. A perfect man like him would want a perfect woman, and that certainly isn't Dixie. But Jake knows a special lady when he sees one, and he's in hot pursuit of her down-home charm and all-delicious curves. If only he can share the secret of why he came to her town in the first place . . . A little mystery, a touch of Southern magic, and a lot of white-hot passion—who could ask for anything more?

A handsome devil of a rancher will send you swooning in THE LADY AND THE COWBOY, LOVESWEPT #494, by Charlotte Hughes. Dillon McKenzie is rugged, rowdy, and none too pleased that Abel Pratt's will divided his ranch equally between Dillon and a lady preacher! He doesn't want any goody-two-shoes telling him what to do, even one whose skin is silk and whose eyes light up the dark places in his heart. Rachael Caitland is determined to make the best of things, but the rough-and-tumble cowboy makes her yearn to risk caring for a man who's all wrong for her. Once Dillon tastes Rachael's fire, he'll move heaven and earth to make her break her rules. Give yourself a treat, and don't miss this compelling romance.

In SCANDALOUS, LOVESWEPT #495, Patricia Burroughs creates an unforgettable couple in the delectably brazen Paisley Vandermeir and the very respectable but oh so sexy Christopher Quincy Maitland. Born to a family constantly in the scandal sheets, Paisley is determined to commit one indiscretion and retire from notoriety. But when she throws herself at Chris, who belongs to another, she's shocked to find him a willing partner. Chris has a wild streak that's subdued by a comfortable engagement, but the intoxicating Paisley tempts him to break free. To claim her for his own, he'll brave trouble and reap its sweet reward. An utterly delightful book that will leave you smiling and looking for the next Patricia Burroughs LOVESWEPT.

Olivia Rupprecht pulls out all the stops in her next book, BEHIND CLOSED DOORS, LOVESWEPT #496, a potent love story that throbs with long-denied desire. When widower Myles Wellington learns that his sister-in-law, Faith, is carrying his child, he insists that she move into his house. Because she's loved him for so long and has been so alone, Faith has secretly agreed to help her sister with the gift of a child to Myles. How can she live with the one man who's forbidden to her, yet how can she resist grabbing at the chance to be with the only man whose touch sets her soul on fire? Myles wants this child, but he soon discovers he wants Faith even more. Together they struggle to break free of the past and exult in a passionate union. . . . Another fiery romance from Olivia.

Suzanne Forster concludes the month with a tale of smoldering sensuality, PRIVATE DANCER, LOVESWEPT #497. Sam Nichols is a tornado of sexual virility, and Bev Brewster has plenty of reservations about joining forces with him to hunt a con man on a cruise ship. Still, the job must be done, and Bev is professional enough to keep her distance from the deliciously dangerous Sam. But close quarters and steamy nights spark an inferno of ecstasy. Before long Sam's set her aflame with tantalizing caresses and thrilling kisses. But his dark anguish shadows the fierce pleasure they share. Once the chase is over and the criminal caught, will Sam's secret pain drive them apart forever?

Do remember to look for our FANFARE novels next month—four provocative and memorable stories with vastly different settings and times. First is GENUINE LIES by bestselling author Nora Roberts, a dazzling novel of Hollywood glamour, seductive secrets, and truth that can kill. MIRACLE by bestselling LOVESWEPT author Deborah Smith is an unforgettable story of love and the collision of worlds, from a shanty in the Georgia hills to a television studio in L.A. With warm, humorous, passionate characters, MIRACLE weaves a spell in which love may be improbable but never impossible. Award-winning author Susan Johnson joins the FANFARE list with her steamiest historical romance yet, FORBIDDEN. And don't miss bestselling LOVESWEPT author Judy Gill's BAD BILLY CULVER, a fabulous tale of sexual awakening, scandal, lies, and a passion that can't be denied.

We want to wish the best of luck to Carolyn Nichols, Publisher of LOVESWEPT. After nine eminently successful years, Carolyn has decided to leave publishing to embark on a new venture to help create jobs for the homeless. Carolyn joined Bantam Books in the spring of 1982 to create a line of contemporary romances. LOVESWEPT was launched to instant acclaim in May of 1983, and is now beloved by millions of fans worldwide. Numerous authors, now well-known and well-loved by loyal readers, have Carolyn to thank for daring to break the time-honored rules of romance writing, and for helping to usher in a vital new era of women's fiction.

For all of us here at LOVESWEPT, working with Carolyn has been an ever-stimulating experience. She has brought to her job a vitality and creativity that has spread throughout the staff and, we hope, will remain in the years to come. Carolyn is a consummate editor, a selfless, passionate, and unpretentious humanitarian, a loving mother, and our dear, dear friend. Though we will miss her deeply, we applaud her decision to turn her unmatchable drive toward helping those in need. We on the LOVESWEPT staff—Nita Taublib, Publishing Associate; Beth de Guzman, Editor; Susann Brailey, Consulting Editor; Elizabeth Barrett, Consulting Editor; and Tom Kleh, Assistant to the Publisher of Loveswept—vow to continue to bring you the best stories of consistently high quality that make each one a "keeper" in the best LOVESWEPT tradition.

Happy reading!

With every good wish,

Nita Taublib

Nita Taublib
Publishing Associate
LOVESWEPT/FANFARE
Bantam Books
New York, NY 10103